# Nice

S0-BNS-979

## Jen Sacks

St. Martin's Paperbacks

NICE

Copyright © 1998 by Jen Sacks.

Library of Congress Catalog Card Number: 98-19407

ISBN: 0-312-96925-2

Printed in the United States of America

St. Martin's Press hardcover edition / October 1998
St. Martin's Paperbacks edition / December 1999

St. Martin's Paperbacks are published by St. Martin's Press, 175 Fifth Avenue, New York, N.Y. 10010.

10 9 8 7 6 5 4 3 2 1

*To Kim, for always being there.*
*To Lisa, for coming back.*

# Acknowledgments

I wish I could say I did it alone. In future, I'll probably claim just that. My thanks to the Inner Circle—Chris, Jules, Janene, E#—some of you for your editorial advice, all of you for just loving me. I needed both. Still do. Enormous gratitude to my agent, Aaron Priest, for taking a chance on an unknown kid; to Lucy Childs, who liked it first; and to Jennifer Enderlin, my editor, for her enthusiasm and patience and for totally getting it, and me. Thanks also to Professor Walter James Miller and his class for getting the gears moving. Nut and Honey, for putting in the hours at my side. Everybody who lent me money (you're in there, Ma). My credit card companies, for staying the course—some of them. And always, always thanks to Victor, the optimist. And to everyone else who believed in me, unnamed but also unindicted. Most especially, the two to whom this book is dedicated.

# 1

## Grace

What is the definition of a sociopath? Could it be someone who's just a little more reasonable than most?

If I had it to do over again (and I didn't know then that I would), I never would have killed the guy in my own apartment. Next time, I promised myself. Don't make the same mistake twice and all that. He was cute, too. It's strange, really. The guys I find attractive in movies and magazines are seldom standardly good-looking; they usually have more character than prettiness in their faces. Yet, somehow the ones I actually end up going out with are typically quite attractive. I just think that my ideal man wouldn't be cute. I'll know him when I see him.

Clayton's deep blue eyes stared up at me, appearing to ask for something he certainly wouldn't know what to do with now. His dark brown hair was so short that not a strand was out of place despite his struggle. He was the first man I'd slept with who actually had a washboard stomach. I've slept with men who had once had them and men who had never had them, but never before had I hit one at the right moment in his life. All too often, men with stomach muscles like that are a little too interested in the perfection of their bodies to appeal to me. Clay, I think, was just very athletic, and his body still held that college-era flawlessness.

Looking at him lying on the bed, the drool from his mouth staining the pillow I'd used to suffocate him, was just depressing me. It's not like he was tiny and easily movable. I sighed and wandered across the apartment to the bathroom. I had about forty lipsticks in a little box that really needed to be sorted. There were so many, some dating a decade back, to college. I grabbed the box and a hand mirror and plopped myself down on my couch, where I was able to keep an eye on the corpse. Just to keep in mind the reason for the exercise. I've always found that applying makeup helps me think things through. I don't know why. Maybe the stillness and concentration on a single activity clear my brain from whatever chaos is disturbing it. I had gone through about seventeen lipsticks—dividing them into pinks, reds, beiges, and other—and my lips were beginning to feel a little raw from the wiping-off process when, even more quickly than I expected, the brilliant idea arrived.

. . I studied the corpse and set to work. When it was found at around 7:00 A.M. that morning just a few steps from the front door of my building, only about three hours after I'd dragged it quietly out of my apartment and laid it there, the police automatically concluded that this was yet another tragic homosexual slaying. New York had seen many lately. That perfect body, clad only in boxer shorts, the freshly cut hair, that handsome face, and, most importantly, the makeup that adorned it—a little eye shadow, a touch of blush, red lipstick—well, what else could they think?

A policeman came around two hours later, making his way through the apartments in my building, asking if anybody had seen or heard anything. I said I hadn't. He didn't seem to suspect me of anything or pay any more attention to me than to anyone else. Very quickly, he passed on to the next door on my floor. There was no obvious evidence

connecting me to the event. Clay's clothes—
big shirt and baggy jeans, now in my closet—
could just as easily be mine. And now were.

Fingerprints? Sure, I probably left a ton all
over him. But my prints aren't in any file
anywhere. Though I certainly didn't intend
to press my luck in the future.

It wasn't either him or me. It was either him
or hurting his feelings. And I've never been
able to do that. I'm empathetic to a fault.

My judgment was off the first night I slept
with him. I was very tired and strained from
work, and his interest was so flattering and
encouraging. I'd met him only a few days
before at a bar—not the usual practice with
me, but it was a very comfortable meeting. I
didn't feel any sexual attraction to him, but I
could see that he thought I was pretty. We
were just joking around, cracking wise about
the trial of the century—the O. J. Simpson
murder trial. We were engaged in a can-you-
top-this contest, and we were both firing on
all cylinders that night.

You know how sometimes two people can
bring out the wit in each other, driving each
other to new heights of brilliance, or so it
seems to them? We didn't really have an
audience—the bar was so crowded and
noisy—but we could hear each other, and
that was all that mattered. With that night's

trial wrap-up playing silently on the TV in a nearby corner of the room, we couldn't help putting words to the pictures we saw. Of course, you can never remember the jokes later, but at the time we were both David Letterman and Dennis Miller rolled into one. Well, two.

And we didn't go home together. I had to give Clay credit; it was a classy move not to put the moves on me that night. He just asked me to dinner "sometime." And yes, I said yes. So it was partly my fault. Because I didn't think I was attracted to him that way. But what do you say at that point? "Well, unfortunately for you, buddy, I can see right now that I will never want to sleep with you or get involved in any way, so the answer is no." Maybe I should have. If I could have, I would have. I like to think that someday I will. But everyone wants to see me date more, because it's something I've avoided for most of my life, filling my time instead with books and work and sex with friends.

I should give him a chance, the chorus in my head said. After all, maybe as you get to know him, something will build to something. And anyway, I've dated so little, I just plain don't know how to turn down a guy when he asks. This little bit of knowledge, which I assume is possessed by more experienced women, could have saved quite a few lives in the near future, but I didn't have it. So I said, "Why not?" He took that as an affirmative.

There are a million things to do on a date in New York. He wanted to cook dinner for me at my place. Did he think that meant we would sleep together? Well, I'll never know now. To tell you the truth, I wasn't all that enthusiastic about this plan. But he had his heart set on whipping up the perfect cold sesame noodles for me. I must have said something to give him the impression that I liked them. Who listens? But I didn't really want a relative stranger in my house. Nobody wants to be raped. Nobody wants to be bored, either. When someone else is in your house, you're the one who's the prisoner.

But, witless me, I told him "okay." They were good noodles. And we didn't sleep together; lying, I told him I didn't do that until I knew someone very well. Actually, I'm weak when it comes to the flesh. He gave me a long, slow, and surprisingly professional massage, but it stopped there, and when I'd put in enough time, I kicked him out. Well, I told him it was time to leave. So he left.

But he called the next day to plan when we would see each other again. That was when I began to hate him. I felt trapped. I just wasn't attracted to him—but, then again, how was I to know for sure until I'd spent a little time with him? And if it turned out that he had had a great time, how was I supposed to tell him I hadn't? I'm not saying there are no ways; I just don't know them. I put him off for a few days, but he was persistent. So I saw him again. I did not give him any encouragement, but he took me back to my place and started kissing me—and it did feel good; it often does. And then he started touching me, and that did, I confess, feel pretty good, too.

But I knew I should somehow have stopped him. He would have stopped if I'd told him to, but I felt it was so unfair to him. I'd let him get all excited, and what was I supposed to do then? Tell him I just wasn't attracted to him? I mean, come on. Who can say that to a nice guy? And he was nice: sweet and well-intentioned and clearly in like with me. So I let him take me there. Or try. I didn't really get there. In fact, I'm not sure where he thought he was going. It's always a problem the first time with anyone. But physically, it felt good—until about halfway through, when even the physical pleasure deserted me, overwhelmed by my urgent desire to be away from him, away from someone who couldn't read the signs, who couldn't see what I wouldn't say.

As he bounced along, I thought to myself, Jesus, what am I going to have to do? Kill him? There seemed to be no other way. It's hard to believe now, I know, but I didn't really think then that I would.

The conventional wisdom has it that guys see sex as just emotion-free pleasure and girls attach too much meaning to it. I wish. In my experience, nice guys seem to want more from me than an orgasm. Clay, for example, kept trying to look me deep in the eyes as we were in bed. His eyes held nothing for me, except for "the look." The look is when a man's eyes soften and deepen and seem to be trying to gaze into your very soul. A very lovely kind of look—if you feel the same way. Once in my life, I welcomed the look and even met it with one of my own. I was sixteen and the boy was the kind of dream date I have yet to stumble into again. Of course, even though he was the one who said he loved me first, when I was just reveling in the sensory pleasure of heavy petting, he woke up from the dream about three months later, after I had convinced myself that love was what I felt, too. A sweet memory nonetheless, as long as I forget the year of misery and confusion that followed, as I tried to understand the incomprehensible: why he'd loved me and why he'd stopped.

Still, you never forget that look. And I didn't really want to see it on a guy I'd met less than a week before, a guy whom—halfway through the event—I wanted not more, but gone. I borrowed a trick from a casual sex pal of mine and squeezed my eyes closed and my face together, as if I was pouring all my concentration into the act. But he kept trying to look me in the eye. He ran his finger along my face and pushed random strands of hair back off my forehead—everything you want a man to do, if he's the man you want.

He lay beside me afterward, apparently deep in thought, his arms around me, kissing me softly on the neck now and then. Leave, leave, leave, I silently invoked, as if it were a magic formula, hoping it would make him disappear. But he was still there. He was a stranger to me, and he refused to admit it. He must have thought that the sex had brought us together. For me, it only confirmed that we were very far apart. It wasn't even a question of technique that I could have given him guidance on. We were just in two very different places—which happens a lot with new partners. He was where he went, and I was still here. The problem was, he didn't seem to know it.

"Well," I said.

He looked at me expectantly, stretching comfortably, as if feeling quite at home.

"I hate to say it," I said, practically singing inside at the happy thought, "but I have to wake up really early tomorrow for work." I caught his look of shock but ignored it. "We're in production on the magazine."

"You mean I can't stay?" he asked, stunned.

"The thing is, I really don't sleep well at all with someone else in the bed. It takes a long time to get used to a person. And I just can't tonight."

It was true, but did he have to believe me? Couldn't he think I was trying to get rid of him, and get the message? I guess not. He called me the next day at work. I avoided setting a date for our next tryst on the basis that production entailed long hours, often late into the night, and I just couldn't plan. He said he'd call in a couple of days.

What the hell was the matter with him? Couldn't he be like other guys? I mean, I'm no prize. He just didn't know it because nice guys bring out the nice in me, despite myself. He thought I was sweet and interested in him and supportive and considerate and enthusiastic and a little bit funny, just because I behaved that way with him. That isn't me. But how could he know that? It's my fault. It's a tic, a habit. Something I can't seem to control. And he would end up paying for it.

# 2

## Sam

The key to a good eavesdropping system is how well it can pick up particular voices in a crowd. Directional mikes and well-placed bugs, now as tiny as a fingernail, make listening in on targets in an apartment, hotel room, or car astonishingly easy. But people meeting in a bar are quite another story, a real challenge. In between jobs, I like to test out the latest equipment myself, naturally in the most difficult of circumstances. The wireless setup I was wearing consisted of a tiny earplug and a Walkman-sized pickup device that used microwaves to pinpoint a desired sound. Politically Correct had not only an eighteen-foot bar and at least thirty small tables but also a bank of ten video screens scattered around the walls, emitting at a level of at least a hundred decibels. I half-expected that the little piece of illegal technology in my pocket would go haywire in these surroundings. The only drawback to the location, though I had chosen it for its unique mix of mechanical and human challenges, was that Upper East Side bars infested with twenty-somethings so rarely produced conversation worth listening to.

I found my eyes wandering as I played with the dials in the right-front pocket of my sports jacket. A couple stood at the bar, talking intensely to each other, with many gestures toward the nearest TV monitor. Whatever was playing, they seemed to be enjoying it. The man was a fairly typical example of the local regular, good-looking in a rather bland way, maybe five-eleven but skinny, with striking blue eyes that did not dart around looking for something better, as so many do. They were fixed on the girl next to him. She was not typical. She did not act as if she were beautiful. She seemed to lack that self-assurance, that coldness. Her face was much more expressive than those of most of the women around her. She was a redhead—convincing, if not natural—with pale grayish eyes. Her face was soft, almost round; her cheekbones were barely differentiated from her flesh. In straight jeans and a simple, tight-fitting long-sleeved cotton jersey, she was slender, with not very much in the way of curves. She was far from perfect, yet she was, in fact, beautiful, just not obviously so. She had warmth, which I found, for some reason, intensely appealing. She seemed very—for lack of a better word—real.

What was also unusual, I noticed as I tuned them in, was that she was talking as much as or more than he was. The typical technique is to let the man hold forth, as we so often do at the least provocation, something a female colleague of mine had once pointed out. Consciously or not, that was clearly not her way. I listened to them for approximately thirty minutes; then one of her friends, apparently, turned to her and drew her back into their earlier conversation. I saw the man write down her number and, shortly after, leave. Now that she was alone with her friends, her demeanor changed markedly. Her mannerisms were boyish, and her constant wisecracks were nasty and much funnier than before. Her friend Marie was black, dressed in black; a little hard-boiled-looking, she seemed like a born New Yorker. The other girl looked a bit like Audrey Hepburn and was just as thin. I did not catch her name. They were smoking with the zeal of Eastern Europeans. Seeing them together, I could tell that they were older than the crowd in general and definitely not, based on their clothes, hair, and manner in general, from this part of town.

A little later, I was not in the least surprised to see the cab I was following drop first one, then the other, and finally the redhead off at East Village apartments.

I am a professional stalker, in a manner of speaking. Stalking is a vital part of my job, and it was easy in this case. The redhead's apartment faced the street, and her curtains were sheer. I decided to continue the exercise the next day. I do not know why. She was not my type. In fact, she seemed quite innocent and normal, if maybe a trifle more interesting than the average. I told myself it would be a nice test run to keep in practice. I would study her habits as if she were a target. I had never taken something like this so far before—I never mix business with pleasure—but I could stop anytime I liked. She certainly was not my type. I was sure that if I engineered a meeting, we would have nothing to say to each other.

# 3

## Grace

After closing the door on the policeman, I walked directly to my bed and lay down. There was no ghost there, just the vaguest memory of how the night before had begun. Clay's calling me up "to chat" and see when we could get together, my putting one obstacle after another in the way, until he said he'd be doing an errand in the area and would like to stop by "just for a minute" to say hello. I didn't know what to say to stop him. I hung up the phone, quietly enraged. He didn't care how I felt. I hated, hated, hated him. I had to change my clothes; I had to wait for him; the evening wasn't mine anymore. Why couldn't I have said, "No, I don't feel like it tonight"? Because it would have hurt his feelings, I just knew. I could imagine too well how it would make me feel.

I dragged off my dirty sweats and put on a red sweater and jeans. I tried to watch TV while I waited.

"Hey, how are you? It's so great to see you," I greeted him after buzzing him up. My tone had all the warmth I didn't feel.

His face lit up as the cold air on his jacket and his arms enveloped me. What am I going to do with him? I wondered. He gave me a couple of gentle kisses and then started smooching my neck. I guess he'd noticed how I'd responded to that before. He walked me over to the bed, this bed, and sat me down on it, running his hands over me. I felt so bad, I hugged him back and let him make love to me. I wasn't particularly enthusiastic, but he didn't seem to notice.

It was late by the time he finished, and he fell into a deep sleep.

He barely struggled, and you know why? He couldn't believe it until it was too late. My knees were on his arms and the rest of my weight on his chest, but he didn't fight very hard. It was amazing. It was so easy. It could have been a terrible mess. I know I was lucky.

Or maybe not.

What is the difference between thinking and doing? What is the line? I didn't think. I swear

I don't remember thinking. And I didn't feel bad at all on this bed. I felt nothing. I forgot about going to work. I closed my eyes and slept for twenty-two hours. When I woke up, refreshed and free, it was 7:00 A.M. Saturday morning.

# 4

## Sam

One of those vicious plastic grocery bags had been dogging my steps, threateningly, for the last two blocks as I strolled, with the wind, down the street to her place. I had been called out of town for nearly two weeks, so I had not seen her since the night in the bar. In a way, I had been glad for the summons, although it only allowed a short time to plan and carry out; it was not really a good idea to shadow her for no official reason. I felt I had been saved from something. Or maybe just delayed.

Fourteenth Street at five in the morning had an almost European feel: the broad sidewalks, the rare solitary person. I meant only to pass by her apartment, to get a sense of her sleeping presence. The Madrid assignment had gone well, despite the haste with which I had had to formulate an approach. It had looked like a typical car accident, a blown-out tire on a curve. The target had had a tendency to drive fast. It was a simple mechanical arrangement. No body to dispose of, even. Yet it should have been enough to take my mind off of her. It had not.

I was the first to see the body lying in front of the building, nearly naked on the street. So undignified. For a moment, I was worried about her, but her building was quiet. The corpse seemed to have just appeared there. But I knew it would not remain unnoticed for long. I brought out my microbinoculars and studied it from across the street as I leaned against a tree. The makeup was confusing, but it did not disguise his identity. It was the boy from the bar.

Odd, I thought. I had not been surprised when the leaders of my former directorate, the one that officially did not exist, had attempted to terminate my employment without resorting to a retirement plan. No newly democratic Russian official wanted my memoirs published in the post-Soviet world. Nor had I been surprised when three of my closest colleagues had turned up dead, the apparently random victims of burgeoning Moscow street crime. That was the sort of approach to be expected from the thuggish mind-set of our former bosses. It would have taken brains of our caliber to contrive more accidental-looking fates. And I had certainly not been surprised to read in the newly freed press of the demise, by stroke, heart attack, drowning, and apparent suicide, of those same bosses, eulogized under their official titles. I had arranged their permanent departures before leaving my hometown forever. There is little that shocks me about death anymore.

But I was surprised to see this boy lying lifeless in the street. I do not believe in coincidence. Do I believe in love at first sight?

Now I felt I had to watch this girl. Either she was in danger or . . . What? She was certainly no professional. Not like any I had known in twenty-five years of creative assassination. Perhaps this was sheer natural talent. Perhaps I was jumping to conclusions because I was a jaded killer with little imagination for anything else. But I had to know.

I left the area immediately. The police would find their way there soon enough. Hailing a cab from several blocks away, I made my way back to the loft I maintain in TriBeCa for my sojourns in New York. I own two floors in the building: I inhabit the top floor, keeping the one beneath as a privacy and security buffer. Before the sun made an appearance through the 18-foot windows on its east side, I was deep in research on the computer, coffee by my hand. All I had had to begin with was the name and address from her mailbox, which I had checked that first night.

I obtained nothing interesting from her Department of Motor Vehicles record or her telephone records (except the relatives she called long-distance). Her credit history was slightly more interesting: too much credit, a few late-paid bills, nothing outstanding for her generation. She was thirty. She was an Ivy Leaguer who had spent the first five years out of school doing nothing much, and she had made very little money at it.

She was now a managing editor of a specialized political/economic journal. She was listed in the Nexis database. I was impressed; she had written several articles on international espionage for her magazine. Now, *that* was fascinating. She had written about corporate drug lords in Colombia and spies who refused to come in out of the cold in Eastern Europe. Her magazine's coverage of the end of the Cold War had been excellent; a little on the paranoid and suspicious side, which was, I knew, not inappropriate. But the bulk of her work had to do with emerging economies around the globe—not the typical purview of an East Village denizen.

She seemed to be a more serious person than she looked; or else she simply did what she had to do to earn money.

There was little in Nexis or anywhere else that documented her romantic life. Her extensive traveling seemed to be work-related. She was unmarried. She paid her taxes on time. She had no police record.

Nothing I found explained that body, but if she had had something to do with it, the reason was unlikely to be in any database anywhere. While I was on-line, I moved some money around, spreading my latest earnings among several offshore accounts and checking on my stock holdings.

I decided I would have to get my car out of storage again. The rest of the research would have to be carried out in person.

## 5

## Grace

I try to be fair, but my boss just plain hates me. I don't know why. I never answer her back. I do good work, though it's never good enough for her. I'm conscientious to a fault. I'm always the last one to leave during production—although that's usually her doing. She lets everybody else go but keeps me, sometimes until two in the morning. I can't think of anything I have that she could be jealous of (except, as one colleague says, a personality). I'm taller than she is; she's pretty short, but she doesn't seem bothered by it. I really don't know.

But no matter what I produce, she can always think of something I didn't do: some question I didn't ask when it's a story of mine; some hole I missed when I'm editing someone else's. She's mean, and sometimes she even makes me cry (not in front of her, though).

She was not happy about the day I missed without calling. I had told her I had such a wretched and constant vomiting illness that I couldn't even think of picking up a phone, but she kept making little digs at me throughout the Monday I came back. I had a lot on my mind. Two stories were late coming in. Another story was a mess that would have to be totally rewritten. And a story I was supposed to write hadn't happened because I had been unable to reach anyone. It was time to switch from the assigning editor persona to the harassing role, but I was the one who was being constantly harassed.

And to top it off, my voice mail wasn't working properly. I wasn't getting all my messages. Fortunately, I had caller ID. Unfortunately, it only gave me numbers, not names. And I can't help it—I need to know. Usually, I recognize the numbers I see or I look them up on my database and find out who it was, but not always. So I called a mystery number up to see who it was. I don't know what was going on, but I felt unequal to actual conversation. Since I didn't know who it would be, I couldn't prepare. As soon as a voice came on identifying the firm I had reached, I hung up. Damn. Now I felt really bad. I hate it when people hang up on me, and that's just what I'd done. I worried about it for at least five minutes, but I couldn't go on to the next task with this niggling at my mind. So I called the number again and got what sounded like the same receptionist. I told her I had just called a few minutes ago but had gotten cut off, although, as it turned out, it was the wrong number. She just responded with a simple "okay" and got off the phone as quickly as she could. She must have thought I was pretty weird, but at least I felt a little better about the whole thing. Because I really had to get back to work.

I suppose, if I had had the time, I might have been feeling some residual guilt and remorse about Clay, but frankly, I wasn't. I had too many things to think about. And that problem was resolved. Obviously, I would not let that happen again. If I ever do go out on a date again, I will not hide my feelings, I vowed. I will not lead anybody on.

Speaking of leads, this first paragraph was definitely not working. I was bent intently over the computer keyboard, trying to salvage some morsel of convoluted text, when one of our foreign correspondents peered over the little cubicle wall of the bull pen and tapped me on the shoulder.

Saved. Pete was in town and he had a

story that could replace the one I never did. Another on-the-spot deal from Lima. Pete worked for us and other publications fairly regularly. He had practically taken up residence in Peru over the last year, emerging from it occasionally to pick up bagels and see his mother in New York. He was fluent in Spanish, and his stories had a forceful, decisive quality that he completely lacked in person. Still, he was okay. We were friendly. Actually, he would often look at me with puppy-dog eyes and indicate in some mushy, indirect way that we should go out. He was not bad-looking, just kind of negligible, not completely there. Not thrilling, not impressive, kind of wishy-washy-seeming. The opposite of his work and his calling.

Nonetheless, I wouldn't have minded chatting, but the wench—that is, the executive editor—had been on my back all day, and I couldn't appear to be having a good time. So I agreed to have dinner with him the next night to catch up. It was *not* a date.

I couldn't believe I was in bed with him. What was I fucking doing? Or rather, what was I doing fucking? My God, had I become some kind of magnet? Now I am irresistible. Now they smell something that drives them to me.

This was a bad idea. This was a bad idea

simply because we worked together. This
was a bad idea because I was not in the least
bit interested in him. This was a bad idea
because I got stupidly drunk. And there
were other reasons, too.

He kissed my neck. He kissed my breasts.
If only he had kissed me on the mouth, I
might have stopped in time. I do draw the
line somewhere. The alcohol or some kind
of intoxication made me temporarily
insane. I was turned on. This, I know, was
because there was no possibility of a relationship. He was at least safe in that
respect. He didn't even live in this country.
I had only to worry about the moment, at
least.

As we moved from the couch to the bed, I
could see that he was visibly aroused. I have
to admit, I'm a little strange about this. I'm
always worried about guys. I think it must
be terrible to show what you're feeling
despite yourself. I hold back a lot when I'm
with men I'm just friends with because I
don't want to excite them accidentally and
make everybody embarrassed. Yet when I'm
close to a guy in circumstances where he
might very naturally have a hard-on, I can
never tell. Well, they wear jeans a lot and I
can't tell anything when they're in jeans. The
denim is stiffer than they are.

But Pete was in his underwear at this

point; so far, all systems go. And I tried not to be embarrassed.

He continued to remove items of clothing from my body and his own. Yes, I was buzzed. Yes, I was still turned on. But I was beginning to wonder about birth control. This is almost always a problem with strangers. On a sublevel underneath the excitement, as the act grows closer, I'm always wondering when or if the guy is going to bring it up. Do I mention it? Is he even thinking about it? Should he have planned? Should I have?

At this point, Pete seemed pretty imminent, and a little undercurrent of irritation was beginning to flow through me. Whatever else I could say about Clay, at least he had been prepared.

"Um," I began. "Do you have anything?"

"Nuh," he said, slowing down a bit. The impression that I got from him was not so much inconsiderateness as the fact that he was just a lay-it-as-it-plays kind of guy. "Do you?"

I gestured to the little porcelain clown on a shelf next to the bed. He reached over and lifted off the head. That's where the little condoms spend months in uncertain anticipation. He took one out and put it on.

"It's not a problem, is it?" I asked timidly. Later, I would slap my head over this one.

Not a problem? He should have volunteered. Or said something. But I just couldn't help it. I didn't want him to be unhappy with me.

"Uh-uh. No," he barely mouthed, going about his business. Whoops, foreplay was apparently over. Time to get down to brass tacks.

Eyes closed, caught up in his own trance, he drove himself inside me. Too fast and rough for ideal entry. Ideal from my perspective, that is. Then he commenced to pound away. I clasped his arms, trying with the pressure of mine on his to slow him down. I didn't want to speak, because that might have thrown him completely off, and I didn't feel comfortable enough with him to know how he'd react. He just kept on at his own pace, missing my pathetic signals. I bore the assault with fortitude, but I was gradually losing my metaphorical erection. I've just never been one of those women who can calmly and coolly tell a man what to do. I just hope for the best.

By the time he had finished—from the sound effects, I'm pretty sure he had finished—I had lost interest in the whole event. He moved away from me and lay down on his back nearby. Still, I said nothing. It was too late now.

Eventually, he left to go back home to mom. With a smile of complicity that he didn't realize was completely misplaced, he turned to pass back out through my door. He didn't know I was upset because I had smiled warmly at him and acted as satisfied with the evening as he apparently was. Not for the first time. When he was gone, I finished the job myself, although I kept finding myself distractedly thinking about what had gone wrong and what I might have said.

The more crushing regret and dismay would come later. He was not a bad guy, but it had not been a good idea. But we were both grown-ups. It simply was what it was. Or what it almost had been. The key to good sex, as I once heard on a morning television show, is communication. I just wish I could do that without actually talking.

He did not call me the next day. Some girls might have been a little miffed. I was relieved.

# 6

## Sam

They were not holding hands.

This man was a colleague of hers. I had witnessed them both entering and exiting the building that housed her office. I had also witnessed him entering her apartment several nights before. I had not witnessed him entering her, but I assumed that he had. It was two in the morning when he left, and he had that look, not quite a swagger, but a walk of confidence. It could only have resulted from sexual success. He was most unprepossessing in appearance; I could imagine no other reason.

One would think I could find better things to do with my time, but that dead body nagged at me. I wanted an answer. I believed

. that my persistence would pay off. As indeed it did.

"Guess what?" Pete had asked with an insinuating little undertone.

"What?" She had come through quite clearly on her cordless phone, easy enough to tap if you can work out the frequency— and there are only a few from which to choose.

"You might be seeing a little more of me than you were expecting," he hinted confidently.

"What do you mean?" Her tone seemed a little sharp.

"I'm staying in New York for a few months. Not going right back to Lima this time."

Silence for a few seconds. "Really. Why is that?" She sounded neutral, but he did not seem to notice the cautiousness of her tone.

"I'm doing a series for a men's magazine on life there, but I can do it from here. And the editors want me around while they work on it. So I'm gonna be in town for a while." He snickered a little—in anticipation, I presume.

"No way!"

"Way. So what are you doing tomorrow night?"

"Oohh. I'm booked."

"Friday?"

"I've got a thingy I've got to go to." Now she sounded legitimately regretful.

"Saturday," he concluded, not asking. "I want to see you again. . . . Please, please, please, please?"

"That'll be lovely," she said warmly. "So where are you staying while you're here?"

"At my mom's, for the time being. Then maybe . . . we'll see."

"Oops, that's my call waiting. I've gotta go."

"I'll check in with you Friday," he said quickly.

"Okay. See ya."

But there was no call waiting.

What was she thinking? She had sounded unhappy at first, then perfectly friendly.

Her face was rather impenetrable. She kept it turned away from the man at her side. He appeared to be babbling on regardless. Every so often, he would drape his arm across her shoulder, but then she would speed up a little or point to something and manage to slough it off. They were walking on the easternmost part of New York, by the river, downtown, not far from where she lived. It was only ten o'clock on a Saturday night, but the area was deserted. I was approximately

200 yards away, diagonally ahead of them. I had made the choice not to carry directional listening equipment; though useful for such distances, it tends to be bulky, and I was just supposed to be a solitary stroller, after all. As a consequence, I could not hear the conversation, one-sided as it appeared. I could only sneak looks at her face through my microbinox and watch as expressions flitted over it. Concern, then an unwilling smile, minor irritation, and then a closed look, her eyes moving around as if looking for something of which there was no sign.

They were walking slowly; he was on the side of her next to the water. They meandered closer to the river. And then she suddenly reached her hands out—it seemed without thought, but with all her strength. Reached out and, just like that, pushed him over the low guardrail and into the water. It had happened too fast for him to even comprehend, let alone react. I thought I heard his head striking concrete or a rock on the way down. She simply continued walking, and on her face was a look that was one part anger and three parts relief. A murderer's cocktail. But the relief was so pure. After a couple of blocks, she turned west, returning to the street and a taxicab home. The site where he had gone under was smooth and undisturbed. There was no sign of him.

I leaned against a bench, surprisingly shocked. For twenty-five years, I have been striving to attain what she seemed to be able to achieve effortlessly: the perfect murder. Perhaps I had never had the right motivation.

# 7

## Grace

Blah, blah, blah, blah, blah. Some people have no sensitivity at all. They just assume you're feeling what they're feeling. I mean, what do you have to use, a two-by-four? He'd had such a great time the other night. He really felt that we were bonding. We've known each other for so long, and now something seemed to be blooming. I just couldn't help myself. It was like sometimes when my dad calls, though he's not supposed to, and he says something so obnoxious that I can't stand it and I feel a physical imperative to hang up the phone. Physically, I had to do it. That's what this was. I know I said I wouldn't do this again. But I couldn't begin to think of what to say to him. I did not have a great time the other night. I did not bond with him. Nothing was blooming. He was looking at me with those big puppy-dog eyes, all brown and moist-looking. How could I say that? I'm really asking.

It was a physical imperative.

This is bad. I know this is bad. This is not good. It is not right to kill people. And killing him was too easy. But, oh, it felt so good just to reach out and push him right out of my life . . . and earshot. Just—push. And he was gone. You know what they need to give— instead of classes on how to meet people, or maybe in addition: an advanced class in how to blow them off. Because as far as I know, what people do is, they lie. And I just don't know how. And what if I did? What if I had told Pete that I'd just gotten a call from an old boyfriend—he wouldn't have known that I don't have any—and that he wanted to get back together and work things out. Pete would have been crushed. It would certainly have hurt him. I couldn't bear to look at his face. I would have hurt him. I would have caused him pain. I just don't know how. I can imagine all too well how I'd feel.

And, anyway, the way he got it, he probably didn't feel a thing.

# 8

## Sam

How does she feel when she wakes up in the morning? I thought from the comfort of my king-sized bed. As I maneuvered a cigarette out of the pack on the night table and lit it, I could not shake a feeling. Professional curiosity. That is what I called it. That is what I would continue to call it, for as long as I could manage.

Did she lie to herself? Did she tell herself that they made her do it? Or did she know? Had the man in the bar been the first? There was no reason to believe he was. But somebody had been. At some point, she had crossed a line. I had crossed that line myself, longer ago than I liked to remember. But I had never killed for personal convenience, for per-

sonal reasons. There had always been orders,
and I had followed them. It was work. And I
had grown used to it. A compartmentaliza-
tion process had occurred early on. Strangely,
it would never have struck me to apply my
well-honed methods to a woman when I was
tired of her. There are plenty of ways to get
that message across.

I have got to pull back, I told myself. This
girl is bad news. Dangerous. What in the hell
is she doing? What kind of person is this?
These questions were not at all based on any
criticism of her actions. They were purely
pragmatic. I cannot tolerate a loose cannon in
my life. Of course, there was no reason to
believe she would be in my life, no reason to
believe she should be. After all, this was simply an exercise.

The streets just above SoHo were always
crowded at lunchtime. I did not stay very far
behind the group of editors as they strolled
to a nearby restaurant from their office. She
was among them. No day off from work this
time. She seemed to be behaving perfectly
normally, judging from her companions.

A man in a high castle. I could not stop thinking of that phrase. A large house, set up on a
hill, surrounded by an acre of grassy land,
broken only by a few handsome trees. An old

oak had stood guard, clearly, for many, many years in the front yard. A white birch demarcated the end of the property along one side. There were three lilac bushes in the back. But mostly the grounds offered open space. Thinking back to my own youth, I noticed that there were very few places for a child playing to hide from watching eyes in the house. It was a typical American suburb, clean and apparently exposed to the world.

The drive had not been an unpleasant one. I have driven these highways many times before—in Czechoslovakia, in Hungary, throughout Europe, in fact. The roads are not simply the same from one end of the United States to the other but all around the world. Endless highways, looking almost exactly alike but for the letters on the overhanging signs. The highways of New York and Massachusetts are no different, only a little more granite along the sides.

Four and a half hours from the city to this small New England town. A pretty village, in fact. The man lived alone. He was divorced, though his former wife lived not far away.

Inside, the house was piled high with books and old newspapers and magazines, the master bedroom particularly. There were three smaller bedrooms, once clearly occupied by children, to judge from the artifacts left behind—now abandoned except for some scattered piles of reading matter that seemed to have crept in from the man's bedroom down the hall.

The house was also filled with antiques, mostly Asian; good, if not great, paintings; and thick Oriental rugs. There were no doors separating the rooms on the first floor. On the second level, only the master bedroom had a lock on the door.

I surveilled the site for three days. No one visited. Occasionally, the man went out on brief errands. Nobody called him. The man was seventy, but he looked much older. Skinny, a hunched-over shell of a man with a balding head. He had a strange kind of energy to him. As I watched him wrestle with various tasks around the yard, I could see he was stronger than he appeared at first glance. He looked grim and distracted. At least one TV set in the house was on at all times.

I found pictures of her as a child packed away in several shoe boxes high up in the walk-in closet attached to the master bedroom. There were many photos of two older children playing, often in the snow, which there seemed to be so much more of twenty years ago. There were fewer of her. She was a beautiful child, honey-colored hair, pale skin, and large blue-gray eyes. She was significantly younger than the others. Were they protective of her? Or did they tease her? I was an only child.

Her mother, his ex-wife, lived in a nearby town, in a fairly modern condominium development. Fewer objects of art, many pictures of relatives scattered more prominently around. She worked, belonged to a local singing group, had no love life. But she had friends and grandchildren. They seemed to keep her busy. Her youngest daughter resembled her slightly, but only in appearance. The mother lacked a certain force of personality that I sensed in the girl.

The houses on the street where the children had grown up, where the father still lived, were set wide apart from one another. There seemed to be little neighborly contact.

What had his daughter been like when she lived here?

I drove back to the city. Back to her. She seemed nothing like him.

# 9

## Grace

I had lain awake for hours again last night. Worrying. One article was still late coming in, and I was going to have to explain to Audrey, my boss. I kept going over and over in my head exactly what I would say to her. Ever since her appointment as executive editor over me, shortly before I met Clay, life at the magazine had gotten worse. I spent hours at night reviewing in my head what irritating comments she had made that day and what I hadn't said in response. To this day, if you want to make me livid, just say to me, in a snotty little voice, "Well, did you ask him?" That was Audrey's line, and there was never a final answer. "Well, what did he say?" My response then to be followed up by the inevitable "Well, did you ask him?" Nothing I did ever suited her, though my previous exec had been ecstatic with my work. Audrey was constantly critical, and I never was able to say anything back to her that would deflect it.

I don't get into fights with people; there's nearly always a way around that. Being conciliatory, framing comments as questions, agreeing on the little things, surrounding a criticism with compliments, turning it into a joke: "It seems . . ." "I think . . ." "Wouldn't it be better if . . ." "Don't you think . . ." "Why don't we try . . ." "I'm not sure but . . ." "That's one possibility, but . . ." Palliatives, modifiers. But, no matter how carefully couched, basically saying, It's okay, I'm cool, swallowing it.

So I end up constantly defending myself to myself in my head afterward. Life with my father was like that. Never a moment's rest, always having to shore myself up, remind myself I was okay. And I hate having the same thoughts go around and around in my head, over and over for hours. Reliving the latest insult and my lack of any decent response.

I guess *I should kill her* would be the obvious thought, but, in fact, it never occurred to me. That sort of thing is worlds apart from what I had been doing. I never meant to kill anybody. And there was too much motive and too little opportunity. But mainly, you can't just murder someone who's making you miserable on a daily basis. A grown-up person finds some reasonable way of dealing with it. If only I could just stand up to her. That would be enough. Instead of standing silent, stunned, hurt, and helpless.

# 10

## Sam

Every person carries the seeds of his own murder in him.

The first step is identification. My target is presented to me (formerly by my superiors, currently by the select few independent clients I have cultivated): photo, name, residence, any background documentation available. Then I begin the research, the most exacting and revealing phase. There are a thousand ways to eliminate someone. The method chosen simply depends on his personal habits and weaknesses and whether the event is to be structured as an accident or a crime. For a message to be sent, the act must be seen to be intentional. To merely remove an obstacle, an accident will suffice.

Home, transportation, lovers—these are the key openings. Medical conditions, hobbies, job—all hold within them life-threatening actions. All I have to do at first is watch. What does he eat? How does he drive? With whom does he have sexual relations? What are his habits and how can they be used against him? It is rarely necessary to crouch atop a roof and fire a long-range weapon. Life is rife with opportunities for death. Most people refuse to think about that. If they did, they could not live. I do. If I did not, I could not kill.

There are a wide variety of ways to watch them, to listen to them, and hence, to analyze them. From the outside, I can know them.

Then I decide what steps to take, how to remove them. I choose the time, the place, the method. They may suspect, some of them, that they are in danger, in a general sense. But they have no idea about me. They may fear the man in the dark with a gun. But not the next mouthful of food. There is nothing I would not be willing to do. I try to keep innocent parties out of it, but, I must confess, occasionally I am not completely successful in that regard. For the most part, however, that reflects a lack of temporal leeway. Given the necessary time, I can accomplish my goal without ancillary damage.

I never worry. I simply watch and act. I have faced particularly challenging cases, but they just require a little more observation and thought. I always know what the ultimate result will be. His death or mine. Most likely, his. It is a liberating sort of knowledge. Little problems seldom trouble me. Methodical and final—both at work and at play—that is my personal philosophy. But it is not one I can ordinarily share.

# 11

## Grace

The man sitting to my right was beginning to get on my nerves. I couldn't help noticing him. His gaze seemed to be fixed on me. Fixated, as a matter of fact. Head tilted toward mine, his face showed expressions that seemed to reflect the conversation in which I was participating. My friends and I were engaged in the typical premovie banter, although, I humbly suggest, more objectively amusing than other people's.

The repertory theater was crowded, as it always is, first because there are so few of them left in town and second because it's so badly managed. "Is that just a coat?" asked a near-desperate person in the aisle, clearly hoping against hope that the seat was mirac-

ulously free. "No, it's Elvis Presley's coat,"
muttered my friend Marie, who is at her least
patient in movie theaters (which is saying a
lot). Her years in New York have not been
kind to her once-midwestern spirit. She
doesn't even escalate anymore. The vilest
curses jump off her tongue at the first hint of
confrontation, and an ugly leap over the
seats is very close behind. This movie theater
is always a disaster, from the mob of people
in the line outside (queue, as the Brit friend
also with us would put it, though both words
were inaccurate) to the masses fumbling for
the few decent seats with any sort of reasonable view.

"We could do it better," I opined to Marie,
Clare (the Brit), and Connor, her husband,
closest to me on my left side. "Bigger screen,
more organized, arrange the seats better."

"And we will decide who will live and
who will die," burst out Marie.

It was natural enough upon hearing this
either to laugh along with us or, just as naturally, to despise our twisted attitude. But the
man on my right just kept on looking and
attending to our conversation, and what I
had noticed subliminally from the first second it began now hit the forefront of my
mind.

It made me very uncomfortable. So I told
myself that he was just waiting for a friend,

and after the seat on the other side of him
was taken, that it was filled by someone he
knew. But that simply wasn't the case. He
didn't look like a pervert. I know what movie
theater perverts look like. My best friend at
college and I had a run-in with one when we
were attempting to see some French comedy
once. That time, shortly after sitting down,
we identified the source of a shared general
sense of unease. The man sitting in the row
in front of us had his head apparently permanently swiveled around, staring at us. We
rose together and moved. He started to follow, so we slipped out of the theater, told
one of the people who worked there about
the guy—as if an usher were going to do
anything—got our money refunded (first
things first), and ran back to our dorm,
where we hunkered down fearfully.

This guy wasn't like the swivel-headed
guy. He looked pretty normal. He was on the
early side of middle age. He just wouldn't
shift his attention away from me and onto
the screen. I sat throughout that whole
movie, part of my brain ruminating on the
weirdo next to me, body at the ready—to do
what, I don't quite know—to defend or
attack should the need arise. But outwardly,
I ignored it. As if it just wasn't happening.

When the lights came on at the end, he still
seemed to be angling for an in on our conver-

sation. I sat and watched every last credit, my head straight forward, staring at the screen, seemingly oblivious to everything else. But peripherally, I could see exactly what he was doing. He was slow to rise from his seat and slow to put on his jacket. Then he stood patiently for a few moments in the aisle before finally appearing to leave. I sat stony beyond that point. Naturally, my friends sat waiting with me. I thought they thought I was really into the credits until Connor said, chuckling, "Gee, weren't you going to introduce us to your friend?"

"Yes, he seemed quite fond of you," Clare piped up. I was stunned. They had all noticed.

"You guys saw it, too?"

"Hard to miss, sweetie," said Clare.

"I just wasn't sure—" I stumbled. "God, he was just driving me crazy." In a way, I was relieved that I hadn't been imagining it. And in a way, not.

Connor looked at me. "I would have switched seats with you if you wanted."

I shook my head blankly. Maybe that would have made it all real. And he had been sitting quite happily with his wife. I would have inconvenienced them.

# 12

## Sam

I noticed him right away. Five foot ten, shaggy white-gray hair, navy windbreaker, khaki pants. From the moment he sat down beside her, it was obvious he was interested. I expected she and the rest of her party would immediately change their seats, although there were not many left in good locations. Still, one would think . . . But she did not even appear to be aware of this man's attention.

I procured a seat two rows behind them, on the aisle. This involved explaining to a relatively weak-minded theatergoer some hypothetical problem with my eyes and the exchange of a small amount of cash, accomplished fairly quietly. I sat, and while she and her friends watched the movie, apparently unaware, I thought about the man. I did not like him. At best, he was pathetic. At worst, a threat. I was not at all sure, despite her murderous activities, that she would be in any way equal to dealing with him should he become obviously dangerous. Her head was steadily turned up toward the screen. People are so oblivious at the movies, so blind to who and what are around them. An excellent place to kill, as a matter of fact. I do not go to films very often, but when I do, I nearly always sit in the last possible row. My view may suffer a bit, but I have never felt comfortable with people behind me like that. It seems to me, with my particular perspective, to be asking for trouble.

How could she be so oblivious? This man was practically breathing in her ear. Sometimes I think I will never understand normal people. I spent the duration of the film tensed and lethally prepared, in case the man became active. I also cast many subtle looks behind and around me.

What a dedicated movie fan she must be. She stayed to watch every last credit, as did her friends. By the time the end titles were through rolling, the white-haired man was gone—out of the room at least; there was no knowing as yet whether he would be waiting for them outside. I knelt, doubled over in my

seat, pretending to tie my shoe, as she and
her friends slowly got up and put their coats
on. I heard her say, "He was driving me
crazy."

As I followed them out slowly, glancing
around but finding no sign of the man, I realized from her swift looks around her that she
was looking for him, too. I had to admit, I felt
I understood her even less now. She apparently *had* been aware of the man the whole
time (or else perhaps it was me of whom they
were talking). Yet she sat in place through the
entire movie, as if the man did not exist. Was
she truly crazy? Had I been denying the evidence to myself?—although in my defense, I
could point out that she had several apparently sane friends.

Why had she not switched seats?

# 13

## Grace

Once upon a time, there was a lovely young woman from England. One day at some gathering, she met a shaggy, young, way-too-intense death-metal guitarist. She didn't think much of him. But he thought about her. He sent her music. He called her daily. Sometimes he would just show up at her doorstep. She pretended to be sick when they met. When he called, she had people say she wasn't there. With either touching or frightening fidelity, he wrote to her constantly. Finally, she consented to go out with him. Not much later, he proposed. When he asked, enraptured, "Will you marry me?" she responded, one eyebrow raised, "Are you serious?" The death-metal guitarist said,

"Yes." To which she responded, quite calmly and Britishly, "All right, then." And so they were married.

They are very happy. It's the one-in-a-thousand stalking that works out well in the end.

But then, she never once said, "Go away."

I suspect that deep down, there was always a part of her that rather liked him from the start. But even if she hadn't, I'm not sure she would ever have said that. It's so hard to do. Another girl I know once had a friend whose ex-paramour never stopped trying to see her. Even after she was engaged, he drove up to her house to see her, and she actually went out to the car to talk to him. This, I thought when I heard the story, is how women die. From being too nice.

We walk down the street and, even though we hear the footsteps behind us, we don't look back.

The half-drunk guy at the bar keeps pestering us. He wants to talk. What are our names? Where are we from? We politely answer, not giving him our last names, but throwing him some conversational bone. We look around desperately to see if our friends have shown up. If we think fast, we make up names. One in a hundred has the nerve to tell him to fuck off. In the movies, maybe, not in real life.

The cabdriver asks me if I'm originally from here. What do I do? he wants to know. I give the most general answers possible, and turn the dialogue to monologue. He works ungodly hours; he is saving money. He used to do double shifts, but he would fall asleep at the wheel. He was last in his country three years ago. It is so hard to meet people here. You are a nice lady. Would you like to go out some night? . . . *Why not? What is wrong with you? You think you're too good for me. You wouldn't go out with a cabdriver?* That has nothing to do with it, I say. I know what you're thinking, he says angrily. I don't generally get involved with people I've just met, I try to explain.

I get out of the cab, shaking slightly, feeling awful. Now he feels rejected, insulted, outraged even. I feel misunderstood. Why do they say these things to me? Why do I try to answer?

I have an acquaintance who can actually say, "This conversation is over. Just drive." But then, she can also say, in all honesty, that she is married. In fact, she's even said, with some truth, "Sorry, I've just given birth."

I can't lie about that. I wish I could. I wish I didn't have to.

# 14

## Sam

This woman is a most puzzling combination. When she walks down the street, there is something almost childlike about her, something innocent. That is, the majority of the time. In sneakers, she carries herself like a ten-year-old. In boots, she moves forcefully. On the rare occasions when she dons heels, she manages to give the impression that she is sexier than any other woman. She does not swing her hips; she glides. Her legs look longer than other women's legs. I wonder if I am being somewhat less than objective.

She never meets anyone's eyes, yet she seems to be looking around her without fear, without special interest. She will not see the men who look at her. She neither hunches nor sidles uncomfortably. When some oblivious moron bumps into her, she says, "Excuse me," smiles. When someone needs directions, if he does not have the appearance of a serial killer, she gives them to him, maintaining her distance, her lips halfway between a lukewarm smile and a straight line (although they curve too much ever to be without expression).

It must be difficult for her, trying to take in everything on all sides, while making eye contact with no one. It cannot be easy keeping her posture in an almost untenable balance—not belligerent, but not weak; not worried, but not unaware.

I can see it because I am concentrating and because I am a predator. I know what to look for, and she tries not to give an inch. Is it a conscious effort every minute, or is it an unthinking habit? Despite the occasional real threat, much overstated in American women's minds, she is not really under siege. In Santo Domingo, the women walk and roll; they ignore the men they pass but expect not to be ignored by them. In Paris, the women revel without thought in male attention. The game goes on all the time; there is no defining line between the streets and the bars.

But in New York, eligible men pay little mind to the beauty they pass on the avenues. There are specific places for that sort of thing.

The men who do appreciate it are not the men these women are seeking. Detached, for the most part, from a culture that supports the back-and-forth of sexual badinage, these men must seem dangerous. Women like her do not know how to respond; acknowledgment is encouragement, talking back, looking for trouble. There is no joy here.

Does she dance, hips swaying, bare feet feeling the floor as if it were island dirt, alone in her apartment when no one can see?

Someday I would like to ask her what thoughts she has as she walks alone through the city. Would she let her body relax and breathe, catlike and free, if I were next to her? Or do I flatter myself too much to think that she would let me do the worrying for both of us? Is it too deep within her? Is she just too dangerous?

Is she right about what some of us are thinking as we gaze?

# 15

## Grace

I don't know what David sees when he looks
at me. I see a big overgrown boy whom I
sleep with every now and then. There's nothing romantic about it. He's a friend I used to
work with. Maybe once a month, we get
together to watch a movie and fool around.
It's been going on now for over a year. God,
longer, now that I think about it. This is, of
course, distinct from the time when we slept
together in the possibility of something
romantic. Sort of. Datingish. But that didn't
work—for him. After about three weeks of
skittishly "going out," I began to think
maybe I might want him around. That's
when he started avoiding me. I chose well,

huh? But that is not the point. Although it kind of borders on the point.

Which is that I don't want to do it anymore. Not that I don't enjoy it when we do. I do—some. But with nothing more going on, it's just sex. And if it's just sex, then I need novelty. Strange. Not the same, meaningless thing. No pun intended. Which is not to say that I don't want to have sex anymore at all. I want to make love: to have sex with someone I love or am in love with, with someone who loves or is in love with me. I remember. I remember how exciting that could be. Skin touching skin sets up that electric charge. Just standing near someone and you feel aroused—and maybe a little guilty. Anyway, I don't know how to tell him.

Yes. So what else is new? Well, he's a very good friend of mine, but this has gotten to be a habit. His feelings will be hurt. Not hurt so much if I say I'm dating someone and I want to give that a full chance. But it's a lie. I hate lying. Not because of the other person, but because I'm not myself. Because I'm shifting myself around for someone else.

Wait a minute. He said that to me once. I can't recall exactly what his words were. We hadn't been doing this very long. He decided he wasn't being fair to his putative girlfriend at the time. Don't ask. And he said—what?

"We can't sleep together anymore." Or "We can't keep doing this." Or "I can't sleep with you anymore." Or "I'm not going to sleep with you anymore." It's right on the tip of my mind—what exactly he said. But I know it's what he meant. I remember, even though I wasn't that into it, that I felt rejected. I did feel rejected. I think I cried a little, although not in front of anyone.

Yet he didn't seem to have any difficulty saying it, whatever it was that he actually said. We? I? Can't.

I survived. Not that he even kept with that program.

So I'll just tell him. On the phone. That's how he did it. And I won't lie.

"David Cane," he says in his business voice. He works at home.

"Hi, Mr. Cane."

"What's up?" His voice is back to normal now.

"Nothing much. Oh yeah. We can't have sex anymore." Hard to believe this slick line is the result of about half an hour of practicing beforehand.

"Huh?"

"I'm not having sex ever again."

"No way."

"Big way. I don't want to." I'm not picturing his face. "I only want to make love."

"Uh."

Not really getting a good sense of his feelings at this point, I say, "We don't do that."

"You know I love you."

"Not that way." I brush it off because I'm right. He means it, but he doesn't really distinguish between loving a woman and loving his friends, which is kind of a problem for his girlfriends, but that's not any of my concern except when I talk about him behind his back to my friends. "It's bad for me. Not the sex. The feeling. It's a bad idea."

"Geez, so . . . out of the blue?"

Don't say you've been trying for a while to say it. "I know. I'd still love to hang out with you and stuff. If you want to still. Not having sex. I mean we used to do that."

"We can try."

"You've got to get a girlfriend."

"You've gotta get a boyfriend."

"I'm working on it." Sort of. "I understand if you don't want to hang with me. But it will hurt." The tenor of this conversation is reminding me of what it was like way back when we were dating. Tentative, a little nervous, no ease. Not the way I talk to him, verbally abuse him now—in every other conversation. When I don't care.

"Hey, what are you gonna do? If that's how you feel."

"No seducing me."

"That could happen." He snickers.

"Don't make me hurt you."

"I gotta go. Bye."

"Bye." But he is already gone. Sounds worse than it is. He always does that. This time, I let him get away with it. It's a habit of his, ending the conversation suddenly. We've argued about it, in fact. 'Cause it's rude. But this time, I give it to him. I don't know what he's thinking. Maybe what I was. Maybe how to seduce me back on my word. Maybe about something else entirely.

But the most important thing is: He lives. Maybe this is a milestone. I really like to keep my friends.

I'm so happy.

# 16

## Sam

I have never heard anything quite like it before.

I had only placed one listening device in her apartment, aside from the one in her telephone. But it was advantageously located. And so I must confess that I did overhear the last time she and her friend David had sex. It was only a couple of weeks after the disappearance of the reporter, Peter, from her circle of acquaintances, shortly after I put the bug in her bedroom, as a matter of fact. After what I had witnessed, I was a bit puzzled by this man's place in her life. But it seemed he represented something like a comfort food for her. Though not, it seemed at first hearing, this night.

I believe that they began in the living room area (a generous description—the bed was just a few steps away), watching a television program. It was a politically oriented talk show, but the guests were celebrities. This did not please her friend, who seemed to have strong opinions, I would guess, on every topic. They both apparently took their TV watching seriously.

"I don't want to hear this."

"You don't want to hear what?" said Grace.

"I don't give a shit what some actress thinks about politics." A pause. Then, more irritated, "These people know nothing, so why am I supposed to listen?"

"What do you mean, 'these people'? These people on the show? Or these people in general in the world?"

"All of them."

"You didn't see Alec Baldwin go head-to-head with Laura Ingraham, that mean young Republican woman. Or Billy Baldwin take on G. Gordon Liddy. Ron Silver's in law school."

"So I have to listen to Barbra Streisand on the budget?"

"No," she said, beginning to sound angry. "You can pick and choose. You're saying that these people as a class, actors, cannot, by definition, have anything worthwhile to say on politics. What other class of people can you say that of?"

"I just don't need to hear it."

"A, they could have something interesting to say. B, it could be amusing just to hear them say something stupid, which is no less stupid if a professional politician says it. C, sometimes they actually say funny things."

"Can we turn this off?"

"What is your problem?" she said, exasperated. "I would like to judge just on an individual basis who has something worthwhile to say. I just think it's ridiculous to dismiss them as a group."

"I don't want to talk about this anymore," he said firmly.

"Fine. I don't want to talk to you anymore, period."

"Let's go to bed."

"You go to yours, and I'll go to mine," said Grace, not sounding as if she were joking.

"C'mon. Let it drop."

"I'm irritated. You can be so unbelievably pigheaded and just plain wrong."

"In another minute, I won't want to stay here, either."

"Fine."

"C'mon."

"What are you, nuts? I am absolutely not in the mood."

The next I heard, it appeared that they had moved to the bed.

"Good luck, champ. I am totally not interested," said Grace.

"That won't last forever."

"I wouldn't make any large bets on it."

A rustling of sheets. The sound of flesh touching flesh, a man's (I guessed) mouth on a woman's skin, as he grunted and kissed. So far only the sounds of one person making love, not two. Grace was laughing softly.

"Stop that. . . . You really don't deserve this."

"I know," she said, chuckling.

"Oh, ha-ha. You don't get treated this well by just anyone. I go to town. I'm going out of my way to give you a good time, to get you to enjoy it."

"Pathetic."

"You are a demon. You know it." His voice was a bit muffled. His head was between her legs now. I recognized that sound. "Ha! You're wiggling," he announced proudly.

"I'm just trying to make you feel your efforts are not being completely wasted."

"Oh, they're being completely wasted all right. I can't believe what I do for you. I can't believe the depths to which I will sink, the humiliation I will endure."

"Yadda, yadda, yadda," she said, laughing harder.

"Stop laughing!"

"God, this is so ridiculous. You'd never do this for a girl you were in love with. This is a battle to you."

"And I'm winning. Look, you're wet."

"Honey, that's from you."

"Don't 'honey' me. It is not. Aha, how 'bout this?"

"No, don't," she half-screamed.

"See, these are the secret weapons. If I can get to these two guys, you are history." Loud lapping sounds.

"Ouch," she said, quietly but seriously. "Too rough."

"Sorry," he muttered.

She seemed to be giving up the fight. I heard quite a few little murmurings, intakes of breath, tiny exclamations. I did not know if she was a slow starter in general or if this was simply a game between them (although I would gamble on the latter), but it did seem that when she let herself, she was quite a little responder. Everything he did resulted in some kind of audible act of appreciation. He grunted only occasionally. Then I heard her cry out somewhat louder; that must have been when he made his frontal attack, abandoning his flanking maneuvers, to belabor the analogy. I could hear her respond every time he drove himself into her. Now and then, he would say, as if in victory, "Yeah, yeah," but mostly he was silent. After some minutes of this, her cries began to sound a little tinged with pain.

"Okay . . . you gotta stop soon," she said, slightly out of breath.

"Uh-huh."

A few minutes more.

"Really." There was definitely an edge to her voice now.

"I know, I know . . . but it feels so perfect. God, I love fucking you."

"Yeah, well, that's why I let you do it. I don't know why you do, but it's sure flattering. I mean flattening. C'mon now."

A couple of loud gulps of air, a small grunt. It was over.

"Well, I got mine," he said.

"Great."

"What happened?"

"You know I'm very clitoral. And when it gets too much stimulation, I can't come."

"Damn, I should have made you come first. But then, maybe I was so irritated with you, I didn't want you to."

"Maybe I was so irritated with you, I didn't want you to."

"Nobody would believe how much work I put in here. How much embarrassment I'm willing to tolerate. As you lie there laughing at me in the midst of my most brilliant efforts."

"If I wanted you to work that hard, you'd never do it. And if I was volunteering for sex, you'd be running."

"Yeah, we really know how to make it work, don't we?"

"You're sick."

"So are you."

"Great comeback."

"Aaahhhh," he grumbled.

Silence for a few moments. I suspect that, without a word, they were cuddling.

"I've got to check my messages," he said.

"Go ahead."

There was nothing exciting there, from my perspective. A few minutes later, I thought I heard him lie back down on the bed, munching something. They discussed the President's China policy for a while. Then they engaged in some idle chatter about former colleagues, as far as I could tell. "So are we seeing a movie later this week?" he concluded.

"Maybe. I don't know what I'm doing yet. Call me if you're thinking of one."

"You call me. I always call you."

"Whoever."

He was pulling on his pants now. "I gotta go," he said in a friendly tone.

"Okay, sweetie. Are you walking home?"

"Yeah. I think."

They were near the door at this point. "Well, be careful. It's late."

"Um-hmm."

"Now, no thanking me," she laughed. It appeared to be a reference to an old joke between them.

"Ha! I wouldn't wish you on my worst enemy." He laughed.

A quick kiss, and he went out the door.

There is something to be said for sleeping with somebody you know very well. They were extremely comfortable with each other. More than most couples involved in a romantic relationship ever get. That is why I was startled when I heard the telephone conversation in which she ended it. Startled, but not unhappy. I wondered if she and I could possibly ever share that kind of ease—at some point after we had met, of course. But I am not exactly confident that that is what I would want. Not immediately, anyway, but perhaps after a number of good years.

No. True lovers can never be that relaxed with each other. There can only be a complete lack of tension when neither one cares. Not that I can claim to know the answer to this inquiry. It had never occurred to me to wonder.

# 17

## Grace

When I opened the door and saw him, it was through eyelashes caked with blood. I didn't know whose. I had heard the knocks—steady, controlled, substantial taps—through a haze. I had had to push Ben's body off of mine, and this was almost as difficult as killing him. I could hear a little rattle from his windpipe as he sank to the floor by my side. My tiny apartment lay in ruins, and now the proverbial knock at the door. The last thing I wanted to do was to open it. It would mean getting up. A voice outside said urgently, "Grace, open the door." Well, if you put it that way. Slowly and painfully, I got up onto my feet and, without really thinking, staggered to the door, unlocked it, and swung it

wide. A man walked in, all business, and—
with no hesitation—closed the door behind
him, turning both locks. I stared at him,
numb, while he took in his surroundings.

Usually, I'm not unhappy to show my
apartment. What it lacks in space, it more
than makes up for in character. A drug-
addicted former tenant had painted the walls
a deep blue and a dark red, with accents in
forest green. There were shelves and shelves
of books, piles and piles of magazines, racks
of CDs and records, a table, chairs, bench,
sofa, big comfy chair, filing cabinets, desk,
oversized TV, stereo stuff, computer, humid-
ifier, two big floor rugs and, of course, a bed.

The charm part lay in how it was
arranged, open and inviting, and in the variety of art on the walls and tchotchkes scattered throughout. There were representative
objects from every part of the world where I
had traveled, photos of the few people I
loved and the many more places I'd been.
Everything in it said "me," from the little
wooden elephant whose original home was a
small village outside of Bangkok to the large
gray candle in the shape of a brain that my
brother gave me one year for my birthday
(from a *Star Trek* episode: "Brain, brain, and
again brain. What is brain? Is brain con-
troller?"). I had Mexican death masks on the

wall and a Matchbox police car from my youth patrolling some books.

I guess the current mess said "me," too.

The man placed me gently in a chair and started to brush me off, so to speak. He seemed to take in far more of my appearance than I did his. All I could really see were his eyes. They were dark and serious. There was something else, too. I wasn't sure exactly what. Some kind of a depth to them, of age perhaps. Maybe even wisdom. That is all I could think at the time, but I wasn't thinking too clearly. He grabbed a little towel from the rack and wet it in the kitchen sink. Then he gently began to clean up my face. Most of the blood, apparently, was mine. My nose had bled from being hit, and in the subsequent melee my whole face had gotten smeared with it. My forehead above one eye felt bruised. There was a little cut on it. And I had sliced my hand on a broken lamp. Aside from that, every muscle in my body felt as if I had just pulled it. I might have.

"Antiseptic?" he asked. I pointed to the bathroom medicine cabinet, just off the kitchenette. He grabbed some cotton balls and a bottle of rubbing alcohol and commenced to make me suffer. As he rubbed disinfectant on my wounds, he kept looking at me, a slight frown on his face.

"You should see the other guy," I offered in an inane attempt at humor.

"I do."

Okay, you talk, then, I thought, irritated.

"When you have regained your composure somewhat, I suggest you take a hot shower. You are still quite disheveled."

Disheveled? Who was he, Jane Austen?

"Then you can get started on cleaning up this place," he added, "and I will get rid of the body."

"Excuse me? I know about being calm in an emergency. I'm usually the one who's calm in an emergency. I mean, I once actually said to a sleazy guy who offered to rape me on a subway platform, 'No thank you,' but—"

"Did you try that tonight?"

"No," I snapped back. "I haven't been to the gym for a while. I thought I needed a workout." Why even try to explain?

"You got one." Nothing fazed him. He stepped back and gazed at the corpse, thinking, I guess.

I could have explained what had happened. I could have asked him who he was and what he was doing here. I could have asked him what he planned to do with the body. I could have asked him why. Instead, I said nothing. It didn't seem to matter to him. He appeared to have his mind made up as to what his next task would be, as if it didn't have anything to do with me. He was an extraordinary person. I knew that from the start. And it had been an extraordinary night. I don't know how else to account for my immediate and bizarre acceptance of him.

Ben was lying on a fake Oriental floor rug in the bedroom area. The rug had some of his blood on it. After a moment's thought, the man went over and wrapped the corpse up in it and, first checking out the window and into the hall, he managed to heft it over his shoulder in a fireman's hold and headed carefully to the door.

"It will wait," he said to me, and left.

And I knew it would.

The problem was that I had told the truth.

I thought maybe it was the men I was see-ing. Writers, actors. I hadn't had the best of luck with them (or they with me). I met Ben, the investment banker, while I was doing a profile of his boss, the head of the trading floor at his bank. My magazine was looking at several of the top traders, and Ben often turned out to be the phone link between me and the Big Man above. He was very funny. Traders usually are. They get all the jokes first: Christa McAuliffe and the space shuttle, Michael Jackson, O. J. Simpson. I found Ben amusing, and he me. I give good phone.

Over the telephone wire, I can be a great combination of sassy and professional. Because I'm not facing the person, I guess, so he isn't quite real. But I had to drop by the firm one day to pick up some photos of our subject, since at our magazine we are always working at the last minute, and there was no time to send them. And that's how I met Ben.

I have to say, from an objective standpoint, he looked delicious. I personally was not interested in trying another date anytime soon. I had had enough of killing, not to mention that awkwardness that seems to be a part of any first date, and besides, one can't count on good luck continuing forever. And however appealing he might be, I knew I probably wouldn't be attracted to him, but I discovered, as he gave me the five-cent tour of the trading floor, that I kind of was. He had a quiet intensity to him, even though he acted the bluff trader. He had close-cropped black hair and high cheekbones. There was almost an Asian cast to his eyes; it added a non-run-of-the-mill quality to him. At about five-eight, he was on the thin but not rock-star-skinny side. At least he filled out his crisp white shirt nicely.

He kept up a patter of investment-banker bullshit throughout the tour, as I got the photos, and as he led me to the door to the department. Then he asked me out to dinner a couple nights hence. I didn't know what to do. What if I actually liked him?

I'm not the only one who isn't what she appears to be. There are others like me out there. Ben was a date rapist, and I didn't know that. If I had, I might have been prepared. I might have even planned to kill him as a favor to the world. But he took me completely by surprise because he seemed so nice.

"Are you okay?" I asked. "You don't look very happy at all." This is where I go wrong right at the beginning. I looked at him with real concern as the waiter handed us our menus.

"I almost screwed up a major deal today. I was, like, this close to being fired."

"What happened?" I asked softly, impressed.

"I basically transposed a couple of numbers, and it was only caught at the last moment. I'm a little dyslexic."

"At least it was caught in time. They're giving you another chance, right?" I looked at him hopefully, and he responded by smiling just a little bit.

"Yeah, but I looked stupid. Which is not the ideal impression you want to give off there."

"Well, you should be in my career, then. It's okay for us to look stupid. Sometimes ideal."

"Look. I don't want to get started on such a down note. Let's figure out what to order."

But he'd brought up his bad luck for a reason, actually. He was lying all the time. I'm sure of that now. And the reason wasn't obscure once I understood the theory. He wanted an edge on gaining my sympathy. He didn't know that nearly every man has that. But I led him to take that approach. Doesn't it sound like I knew and cared about him? I didn't. I'd be a much more successful dater if I didn't notice the other guy's feelings, ersatz or not, at all.

For two and a half hours after Mr. Mystery Man left, I did nothing at all. I couldn't watch TV. I couldn't sleep. I couldn't read. I just sat on my couch and smoked. Even that didn't feel right. I'd be smoking a cigarette and already thinking about lighting the next one, as if the one I had just wasn't enough. When I heard his knock on the door, I felt relieved, I have to admit. I hadn't been worrying about him exactly, just felt uncertain. I let him in and, without saying anything, went back to my couch. He looked exactly the same as when he'd come in the first time— not mussed at all. I mean, I am not an expert on the disposal of dead bodies, but he made it look pretty easy. He came over and knelt in front of me. I had showered and cleaned myself up generally (for some reason repeatedly, almost mindlessly, conditioning my hair); I was wearing sweatpants and a T-shirt, so it wasn't exactly a romantic moment, but there is something somewhat devastating about a man kneeling in front of you.

I expected him to ask me what had happened. I expected that I would tell him, but he surprised me.

"Tell me about the subway," he said, with a slight smile.

I looked at him for a minute, and then I did.

"My best friend in college and I used to move together at the beginning and end of each year, into a dorm, out of a dorm, whatever. We'd always rent U-Haul trucks to do it; each year, the only trucks that were available for us got bigger. Ultimately, we ended up with the two-bedroom-house size. But it kind of encouraged us to feel and behave like truckers. We'd have our sleeves rolled up, cigarettes dangling out of the corners of our mouths, cursing a blue streak. Finally, the move would be over and we'd return the truck.

"The truck rental place was in a fairly sleazy part of town. Because we were college students and didn't have a lot of money, we decided to take the subway one night to get back to school. It was only one stop. But this subway station was unprepossessing at the best of times. What we didn't know as we went down the stairs to enter was that it was also closed. Except it wasn't completely closed. It's just that the turnstiles were fenced off. We knew the subway would stop there. It never didn't stop. But we didn't know how to get in."

He was just looking at me seriously, listening.

"Then we noticed, I think, three sleazy guys loitering down there. And I do mean loitering. Possibly with intent. We didn't act panicked or anything. And one of the guys pointed out a place where we could crawl through the fence. We looked and thought. We could hear a train coming. Diane went first. She bent down almost on her knees, looked through the fence, and started crawling through. One of the men was near her, and as she crawled through, he sort of grabbed at her leg, almost playfully. Playfully, if he'd been someone we knew. Actually, it was scary. She didn't say a word. I thought that was kind of odd. She was always a much more assertive person than me. I mean, she used to get into fights all the time with rude people in the street or in stores. She finished crawling through, got up, and faced me from the other side. Now it was my turn. Two things happened at once. I need to explain that it had been a little chilly outside that night, and I had borrowed and was wearing one of Diane's jackets—a blazer, actually. All her clothes were gorgeous, and she was very protective of them. In fact, it was often a joke with anyone who helped us move that ninety percent of our stuff was her clothes. I can't remember which happened first, but another man, the one next to me, said, 'Would you like to get raped?' At just about the same time, Diane stared at me and said, 'Take off the jacket, Grace.' I looked at her after what the guy had just said, and she just repeated, 'The jacket, Grace.' There was no mercy in her voice. 'The jacket, Grace.'"

I paused a moment in telling the tale, and the man asked gently, "What did you do?"

"I took off the goddamn jacket. Said, very politely, to the sleazy guy, 'No thank you,' and crawled under the fence. And at that moment, the subway stopped and the doors opened, and we went in. I sat down in relief and then looked over at Diane. She had her head down, and I realized she was sobbing. I asked her what was wrong. She just looked at me, and I saw that she had been really scared.

"After she calmed down a bit, she asked

me why I had taken off the jacket. I told her it was because she'd told me to. The fact was, Diane was a very fierce girl, and in the end, I was more afraid of her in the long term, when I would have to deal with what would have happened if I'd gotten the jacket dirty, than I was of the sleazy guy. She thought I was nuts."

"Why did she tell you to take off the jacket?" asked the stranger in my living room.

"I didn't realize this at the time, of course, but at the touch of that guy's hand on her leg, she became truly terrified. Her brain had simply frozen on her last thought."

"The man asked if you would like to get raped and you said 'No thank you.'"

"Yes."

"You realize how inappropriate a response that is to the situation you were facing."

"What are you, a shrink? That's not the point. The point is that I don't get excited in an emergency. I stay calm," I said.

"Were you frightened inside, though?" he asked.

"I don't remember feeling anything at all, if you want to know the truth. Except that I'd be in trouble if I fucked up her jacket."

He said nothing for about thirty seconds and rocked back on his heels. Then he said, "Thank you," and stood up. He stepped over to the big comfy chair and sat down in it, leaning back thoughtfully.

"Who are you?" I asked finally.

"Call me Sam," he answered, if that qualifies as one.

"Sam?"

"Sam."

"You don't look like one," I commented.

"I could say something similar about you," he returned pleasantly.

"I never said my name was Sam," I joked. He didn't laugh.

"Neither did I." He paused to let that sink in, I guess. Then he finally asked, "What happened here tonight?"

"Once upon a time," I began, "I went on a date."

The funny thing is, it was only a midrange dinner, not cheap, but not the most expensive thing around. He paid. I offered to contribute, but Ben refused. I was a journalist and he was a trader and he could certainly afford it, he said. But, you know, since it was, in fact, a midrange dinner, even if he thought paying for it entitled him to some form of recompense, he shouldn't have expected the whole enchilada.

The thing is, I had already killed two guys, and although I wasn't anticipating killing this one, I felt that there was something wrong with my social skills. Perhaps I hadn't tried hard enough to communicate openly.

My apartment felt very small and close with Ben in it. He had walked me home, and so I had invited him in—for a drink, I guess. I only know about this stuff from TV. He wandered around my place while I was making coffee. I felt like Mary Tyler Moore—or rather, like Mary Richards.

When the coffee was ready, I poured it into two cups. Ben came up behind me and put his hands on my shoulders. I felt a little chill, but I wasn't sure from what. He slowly turned me around to face him, paying no attention to his beverage, and leaned down to kiss me. I let him; his lips touched mine, but instead of beginning gently, he forced my mouth open with his own and stuck his tongue in. I let him—for a few moments— but frankly, it wasn't what I'd hoped it would be. It didn't feel sexy, just wet. Still, I allowed him to draw me out of the kitchenette and over to my couch, where we sat together, still physically linked. Then I moved my head back, away from his, and uttered this brilliant line: "Let's slow down a little." What I was really thinking was, Where's the fire, pal? Not here, I can tell you.

"Relax," he responded to my unspoken thought. How unbelievably trite. If you have to tell me to relax, I thought, there's a good chance I'm not in the mood to.

He tried to start kissing me again, but I bobbed my head away when he did, like one of those little duck heads on a stick that children used to play with. I can't help it; that was the vision I had.

"Look," I said. "I'm going to be honest with you. I don't think I feel this way about you . . . at least not yet." All right, I couldn't be totally honest. I knew right when he kissed me that I wasn't interested. I thought it was a shame, but the chemistry just wasn't there.

For a few seconds, I felt great. I'd told him how I felt, and he didn't look crushed at all. Then I didn't feel so great. He looked mad.

Before I could even see him prepare, he hauled off and punched me in the face. This was a mistake. He didn't punch me hard enough. If he had, that would have been that. But it didn't knock me out. I was stunned, even as I thought that a male friend of mine was right—you don't exactly feel the pain; it comes as a blow. Shock is what I felt. I bounced off the sofa and onto the floor. As he leaned forward toward me, I took both my feet and shoved them into his stomach. With an "oof," he settled for a moment back against the couch.

You know how when you're really involved in having sex, you cease being aware of anything else? You have no idea what's on the TV, and sometimes afterward you discover you've got rug burn on your knee or your back, and you didn't even feel it as you were getting it. Technically, it's supposed to be a little like being in a trance: total, tunnel-visioned concentration. This was like that.

Gone were visions of Mary Richards, and instead I thought insanely of Elvira, Mistress of the Dark, in the movie where she's fighting off her evil-demon uncle-in-law. I wished I had a stiletto-heeled shoe like hers to hit Ben with, right in the center of his forehead, but I didn't. Still, I was glad I had kept my cowboy boots on. I had backed up and was about to stand up, with the intention of kicking him again, harder, but he dived at me from the couch.

I tried to twist away, but I didn't make it. He started to climb on top of me, holding me down with one hand on my neck as he began to unzip. I reached toward him with my right hand, looking deep into his eyes and starting to pucker up. His problem was that apparently he wanted me conscious but immobilized. If his goal had been me unconscious and immobilized, he would have done things differently, I'm sure. He hesitated for a moment, confused, while I placed my hand almost lovingly around his neck. Then I pulled his head toward mine and slammed my forehead against the bridge of his nose. It stunned him for a second, and I was able to roll out from under him. I lunged up, intending to head for the door. He lunged up, too, intending to head for me. The long skirt I was wearing tore and got in my way. He got there first and, grabbing my arm, slammed me back into the wall. Near the door, there was a little shelf of stuff that I used to drop things on as I entered my apartment. For a second, it kept me from hitting the wall with my whole body; then it gave way, collapsing.

Backing up with me in tow, Ben managed to destabilize a tall but somewhat rickety shelf of books, which came down around me as he pulled me through the living room. With my momentum toward him as he tugged, I managed to turn to face him slightly and shoved a boot-clad foot really hard into what had been, I assume, his erection. That, I believe, was when his goal changed from rape to murder. They always say you don't want to make an attacker angry; but they don't understand the (very temporary) satisfaction of feeling someone's innards seeming to crumble around a well-placed foot. Anyway, it was just as well that his face got meaner, because at first all I was thinking about was defending myself, which meant I was always a step behind. Now I started to think about how to kill him dead. My thoughts turned to my lovely baseball bat, which I'd bought a couple of years ago for home defense, but it was by my bed, leaning uselessly against a bookshelf.

While he stood stock-still for just a second, in agony, I grabbed for a chair and swung around with it. I caught him on the arms as he moved to protect himself, and the chair kind of went flying, just missing my stereo system. It did bring down a halogen floor lamp. He recovered his balance and leapt forward, enveloping me in a painful bear hug, then dragged me across my small living room, into the bed area and onto the bed. He hit me a glancing blow on the nose and my head fell back, exposing my neck. His weight on my chest, he put both hands around my throat and started squeezing.

I've never been closer to death (my own, that is), and that includes a couple of truly terrifying cab rides. And I knew it. So I did the thing I didn't want to do, even so. It's the most disgusting thing you can imagine, even though all the self-defense experts on TV say you should do it. My left hand was caught under me, but my right hand was free. I jammed my first two fingers into his open left eye as hard as I could. It was as gross as I

feared it would be. I felt jelly. He reared
back, letting go of me, and fell off the bed.
There was goo on his face and my fingers.
Despite the shiver of disgust that washed all
over my body, I grabbed my now-handy bat
and swung it at his head right before his
scream hit the air; it got cut off midroar. His
hands swung out to try to capture the bat,
but he missed it—what with having only one
eye and all.

I jumped off the bed and pounded the end
of the bat directly on his windpipe. I brought
the bat down from the sky right onto it, like a
sledgehammer. I felt the cartilage give, but
he wasn't done. This time, he grabbed for my
legs and managed to knock me down. I fell
on my ass, and as he tried to keep breathing,
he pulled himself on top of me and tried to
strangle me one last time. I wove my left arm
through his and pinched his nose, hoping
maybe that would give him even more trouble getting air in. He seemed to be choking
on something, and I felt his hands loosen a
little, but I think I may have passed out for a
few seconds. I came to quickly, but he was
dead.

I lay, shocked and exhausted, under him
for a little bit. I closed my eyes so I wouldn't
have to see his mangled and bloody face. The
apartment was so quiet. I realized I had completely forgotten to scream.

* * *

Like any normal human being, Sam looked around again at the apartment at the end of my recitation, imagining, I guess, exactly what had gone on where. The corners of his mouth turned down a tiny bit; a thought had passed by, but I would never know what it was.

"I just missed it," he said, almost to himself.

"Do you mean you wished you had gotten the chance to see it, or that you would have helped one of us out?" It was strange, but I had no problem actually expressing my worst thoughts to him.

He looked at me sternly and didn't respond.

"What did you do with the body?" I asked, not unreasonably.

"It is gone," he said.

"Gone as in forever, or gone as in someday to wash up on a beach?"

"Forever." He looked at me. "You do not need to know more than that."

We exchanged glances, and for a second I could swear we had the same thought: The only way I'm safe is if this other person is dead. But that was pretty funny really, 'cause he wouldn't have done what he did if he didn't like me or something, and I would be stuck with a dead body on my hands if he hadn't gotten rid of it. It was only for a second, I think.

"What are you going to tell anyone who asks about him?" Sam inquired.

"Who's gonna ask? It was just a first date."

"If somebody should."

I thought a minute. "Well, if I say I went out with him, then someone may know about his ugly habit and might get suspicious, so I guess I'll say that I stood him up. I was finishing up work on a story and lost track of time."

He nodded approvingly. "I will give that some thought. But it sounds reasonable."

What a character! "I will give that some thought," he says, as if it were his decision. On the other hand, he did seem to have some experience in this nether world of crime. Did he see himself as a possible mentor?

"You are going to be sore tomorrow," he warned.

"I'm a little sore now," I said, but he didn't seem to get the pun.

He looked at me steadily for a while but didn't say anything. He appeared to be thinking. I took it for a few minutes, but then I leaned my head back against the couch and closed my eyes. I started to think, too. I thought about cleaning up my ravaged apartment. Then I started to speculate on other ways I could have killed him. If we'd been in the kitchen longer, knives and other utensils could have been used by either of us. Wait a minute—I hadn't wanted to kill this guy. There's an irony for you. I had opened up and told him what my feelings were. He had not thanked me for sharing. He hadn't cared a bit. I guess at the end, there had been no pretense at all on either of our parts. I was glad Ben was dead. I'll bet everyone who knew him well would be—if they ever found out.

I didn't feel disgusted with myself at the memory of my kissing him, though. I felt disgusted with myself that I had expressed any concern whatsoever about what I realized now had to be that bogus story of his about getting in trouble at work. He must have thought I was the perfect sap. I felt embarrassed. If I hadn't been such a nice, concerned little citizen, worried about a total stranger's well-being, I wouldn't have had a thing to regret.

I smelled something and opened my eyes. Sam was smoking one of my cigarettes. He looked at me through the smoke, and then he actually smiled.

"This is nice," he said softly. I somehow knew he meant just sitting together, quietly thinking.

"You know, you're every bit as inappropriate as I am," I couldn't help noting.

This time, he grinned. He silently finished his cigarette. Suddenly, I felt very tired.

"Are you planning to leave here ever?"

"Ever," he said with no inflection at all, but his eyes didn't look wounded. "Do you want me to stay here while you sleep tonight?" He sounded a little concerned.

"No," I answered.

"Do you think you can sleep now?"

"Yes." My turn. "Are you going to tell me what you're doing here tonight, at some point?"

"Very likely," he said.

We left it hanging there for a few moments. Then I got up and walked to the door. He followed slowly.

"So is this, like, a first date?" I asked archly.

"But you do not have to kiss me good night," he said, and walked out the door.

# 18

## Sam

She may have been feeling no shock, but I was. Shocked at myself for what I had just done.

I had seen what appeared to be two struggling figures through the sheer curtains of her apartment window, and I did not waste a moment. But I had had to break into the two master locks on the outside doors and run up a set of stairs. By the time I stood outside her door, I could hear nothing behind it, just silence. And at that moment, it seemed that all the autonomic systems in my body came to a jolting stop. I thought she was dead.

I know how quickly that can happen. Every little thought and quirk and mannerism and dream wiped out in an instant.

Everything I loved about her, and somehow my whole future, insane as that thought was, gone. When I knocked on the door and called her name, I was more wishing than hoping that there would be a response. Somehow she held a key to me, this girl. Even if it was to a vault no reasonable person would want to open.

I believe I showed no sign of relief when that door opened. My professionalism took over completely. I realize now that I may have struck her as a little on the cold side, yet she did not respond in any way negatively. She was charming, actually. If the man in her apartment had not already been dead, I would have killed him without hesitation.

After all the explanations, I could not keep myself from staring at her. All I could think about was how it would feel to have her in my arms. But I knew I could not act. It would have been in extremely poor taste at this juncture.

I was almost grateful when she finally ordered me out, though I could have sat there much longer, gazing at her silently, pretending that this was a typical evening for us, that we were already lovers, entirely comfortable sharing a quiet moment with each other.

Yes, I could ask myself what in the world I thought I was doing. But I knew, and I am realist enough to accept where I found myself then. I could not think of other circumstances where I would have put myself, with so little to gain, in such a dangerous situation. Disposing of a dead body I had had nothing to do with, revealing myself. But I am human, after all. The motivation: to lie beside her some night after possessing her completely. An inadequate one generally, by my lights, but somehow, in this situation, not entirely ridiculous. A reasonable man must know and accept his own unreasonable side.

I believe I hid my feelings from her successfully—except for my having been there in the first place.

If I had been as intelligent a man as I had always prided myself on being, I would have killed her then. Given my already potentially self-destructive actions, she presented perhaps the gravest danger I had ever faced.

But that is, by definition, love.

# 19

## Grace

I was beginning to think maybe I should start trying to schedule a vacation. The next day, Saturday, I was quite distressed. I mean, this whole thing was starting to take a toll on me. I can't be killing man after man without some ill effect.

That sounds very callous, doesn't it? I don't mean it that way. I'm not going to say that the first two made me do it. I just didn't know what to do with them. But the last one, he did make me do it. The big bully. I showed him. And I can't say that I'm sorry.

I spent the whole day cleaning up my apartment, putting shelves back together, picking up pieces of glass from the remaining rug. It was slow going because, in fact, I was very sore. Everything hurt. It was much worse than a vigorous workout after weeks of doing nothing. Trying to fit my bookshelves back together, I couldn't help thinking that there are certainly times when a man would come in handy. A good man, not a date rapist. Or maybe not so good a man.

Who was he? Sam, I mean. If I closed my eyes, I could see him, sort of. He was tall. And definitely older. Dark, dark eyes and gray-tinged, close-cropped black hair with no part. He wasn't fat; in fact, he was a little on the thin side. Kind of a craggy face. A wide mouth? I know it sounds crazy, but I really didn't have a very specific picture of him in my mind. I mean, there was so much going on, and sometimes when I'm a little distracted, I have trouble really seeing people. I had felt pretty calm at the time, but I had just a general image of him in my brain, so maybe I hadn't been as calm as I'd seemed.

But I knew he wasn't a good man. Maybe good for me, as it turned out. The night before, anyway, but his appearance had raised a lot of interesting questions. How had he known what was happening? Was he just passing by? Please. I don't have that kind of luck. Oh, let's face it, he was dangerous. That's what he was. Probably a lot more than Ben, but the strongest sense I had about him was that he wouldn't do anything to hurt me. It just was his vibe. Not here to hurt you. That's what I got. It was kind of a nice feeling, in the midst of everything that was terribly wrong in my life. There's never been anyone who just wanted to help. God, and I'd been so rude to him. I don't know how I could have been, but it had been so easy.

I did the best I could with my apartment. I was down one lamp, but when I'd finished, that was about it. I had a strange energy that day, given what had happened and the shape I was in, but Sunday, it seemed to hit me.

I couldn't get out of bed until after noon. And then I napped a couple times before dinner. Nobody called. I guess everyone was busy. So I felt strangely isolated. And my face was a wreck. My nose was a little swollen, and the area around the cut on my forehead was colorfully bruised. So was one side of my jaw. It should have been distressing, but I couldn't help looking in the mirror repeatedly, whenever I was awake. This is me, I kept thinking. I was in a fight. And I won. That had never happened before. I'd never fought with anyone in my life. I was a nice girl. It's not that I hadn't ever had the thought, but I had never acted on it. I could get hurt, I always knew. Well, so I had. And here I was.

You know, for over ten years, I'd lived in a

world without violence. Even in New York, none had touched me. But Friday night had gone and changed everything.

"What happened to you?" She said it with a broad smile, almost a grin.

"I got mugged."

"Well, geez, what does the other guy look like?" No sympathy, of course, from Audrey. She just looked amused at my Technicolor face.

You wouldn't want to know, I thought. "You wouldn't want to know," I said coldly.

She looked a little taken aback as I calmly made my way to my desk. It usually took several sticks of dynamite to get her out of her office. Now Audrey followed me to my cubicle.

"Were you able to identify him for the police?"

"I'd never seen him before in my life."

"You know what I mean."

"Oh. Maybe you should phrase your question more specifically."

She raised an eyebrow at me. I would have raised one back at her, but the eyebrow I can ordinarily do that with was in traction.

"It's all taken care of, Audrey. No need for you to worry," I said, looking for the latest version of Pete's copy in its orange folder on my desk.

"Uh, yuh," she said slowly. "Oh, hey, has Pete called in? I had a couple of questions for him on that piece," she said, gesturing with her bagel at the folder.

"I haven't heard from him in awhile."

"Yeah, well, that sounds like him. At least we've got it. They weren't major problems."

"That's good," I said. She went back to her office. I went back to my work. Back to normal, give or take.

# 20

## Sam

I did not let her see me for about two weeks after our first face-to-face meeting. But I saw her. I continued to keep a watch on her. I confess I had no idea what she would do under the circumstances. I was a little concerned that she might react in some negative or self-destructive way to her rather jarring recent experiences. It was within the realm of possibility that she might lose control of her actions—go kill-crazy, in the parlance of my profession. More likely was the possibility that she would confess to someone—official or otherwise—what she had done, or, in lieu of an outright confession, somehow seek out some form of punishment, again via the authorities or perhaps through some means of her own.

Nonetheless, I did not set up any electronic eyes in her apartment because, well, quite frankly, I could not countenance doing such a thing once we had met. I felt a little delicate about it. I even felt rather discourteous listening in on her, now that she was a person I actually knew. If you do not draw the line about that sort of thing, you can lose all contact with humanity. I had seen it happen. For such a person, everyone else ceases to be real; all people are merely targets, jagged lines on a readout, patterns to be assessed and anticipated. In a world like mine, such a path is always a hazard.

But Grace was deliciously real to me. And I no longer wanted to know everything about her behind her back, as it were. I wanted to discover her personality from interaction, not examination. But I kept watch even so, because of my fears, because I did not know nearly enough yet about who she was and of what she was capable.

Yet she seemed incredibly normal in the weeks that followed her violent encounter. She went to work each day. I would see her walk out to lunch with her colleagues. She stayed late at the office often. Occasionally, she would take in a movie with some friend or other—David or, more often, the two women I had first spotted her with. Or she would stay in and read or watch television. She slept alone.

By the end of the first week, her bruises had mostly faded and the swelling receded.

I was beginning to lose my mind for lack of actual contact with her. You see, I had touched her that night when I sat her down to disinfect her wounds. And not since then.

I am only attempting to explain why, after two weeks of such surveillance, I found myself face-to-face with her one evening in a public place, why I had to dance with her that night.

# 21

## Grace

"If you're feeling classical," the club's logo goes. I was, as a matter of fact. Although mostly like a Bach fugue, to be specific. But my friends would not let me off the hook. Classical was the new hot place and I was ordered to put in an appearance.

"You never come out anymore," said Marie.

"I go out more than I should," I said.

"Look, you're supposed to dance at this place. Which I am really looking forward to. But it's definitely a case of the more the merrier, the less inhibited. And all we've done is movies for the last few weeks."

"Emphasis on 'we.' You go out to a club almost every night."

"Yeah, well, after this, I'm gonna stay in for a while and write," Marie promised, faithlessly. I hear this every week.

"Yeah, right."

"No, really."

"Yeah, right."

"You have to come. Connor has promised to dance with every one of us."

"How'd you get him to do that?"

"He lost an argument." She added, "And there are scattered reports that cool guys might be there."

"Heaven forbid."

"Eight o'clock. We'll get there early so we can get a table."

"The most sensible thing you've said yet," I said, giving way.

"Okeydokey, sweetie. See ya there." She hung up.

It'll be okay, I thought. I won't meet anybody. Marie goes out every night, and you can count the number of truly cool guys she meets on the fingers of one elbow.

I got there late because I hate to wait alone. Clare and Connor were already seated at a fairly decent table. Marie was at the bar, for some reason. The place was gorgeous. Brocaded curtains all around the walls, fairly real-looking Louis something or other furniture. The waitresses wore long gowns. It was the opposite of every other place in town: a brilliant idea. The clientele was even mixed in age, but mostly people thirty to forty-five. I don't know about Marie's notion of meeting men, because most of the people there seemed to be in couples or groups. And wonder of wonders, there were actually people dancing to the classic and obscure collection of waltzes the DJ played. The lighting was very gentle; the price of the drinks was pretty harsh. But it was worth it.

Clare and Connor danced together first. Clare was wearing a long, full green taffeta skirt with a tight, pale yellow T-shirt. It was a beautiful sight. I gazed at them dancing and found myself settling back into my chair, half watching them, half daydreaming, mindlessly. Despite all the activity around me, or maybe because of it, I felt a kind of peace. The only disturbance was when Connor insisted on taking me out on the floor. The last time I had touch-danced was several years ago on a business trip to New Delhi, of all places. With a coworker. It felt a little awkward dancing now with my friend, just because we normally have a cat-and-dog relationship, bickering warmly when we get together. And I guess I just felt strange being in a man's arms, although I was glad we were not dancing the way he and his wife had. My right hand was in his left and his right hand touched me only lightly on the back. We were mostly looking at each other's feet, trying to match our steps.

"I think what I should do is step on your feet," I suggested.

"Why would you want to do a thing like that?"

"That's the way every little girl learns to dance. Standing on her dad's big shoes as he swings her around. That's what I'm used to," I explained, smiling.

Connor smiled, too, very warmly. And he said sweetly, "If you do, I will have to kick you. These are new shoes."

"Well, it's the thought that counts. We'll get through this somehow."

"I'm enjoying this, except for the company," he joked.

"I think I need more practice."

"Well, that can be arranged. The night is young."

"But I am old," I said as the music ended and we wended our way back to our table. "Thank you, sir," I added, curtsying in my long black satin skirt. I had bought it at a thrift shop years ago but had never had occasion to wear it.

"A privilege and a pleasure," Connor replied, affecting a bow as he extended his hand to Marie.

I was actually a little winded from the stress, but before I could sit down, I felt

someone come up behind me. He took my
arms and swept me back to the dance floor.
I'm sorry, there's no other word for it. I was
so stunned that I did nothing as he took my
hand in his and, unlike Connor, put his other
arm around me quite solidly, pulling me in
to him until our whole bodies were touching.
It was Sam. He looked down at me, and I
made the mistake of looking back up at him.
Somehow, he held my eyes there; I couldn't
even think about how I was moving, but I
didn't have to. The effect was the same as if,
indeed, I had been a little girl standing on my
father's shoes. An incredibly hypnotic waltz
was playing; it struck me as being half dance,
half carnival. It built, if you know what I
mean, into something more and more dra-
matic, like a ballet. I shouldn't have looked
into his eyes; he wouldn't let me look away,
it felt. And we spun and we spun and we
spun. And I felt dizzy—and breathless—in
his arms.

"It is called the 'Masquerade Waltz'" was
all he said. And we just turned and turned
around on the dance floor, and everything
else was a blur. That waltz was, in fact, four
minutes and eleven seconds long, but it felt
as if I were in some timeless place. I could
feel his large hand around my much smaller
one, and the warmth of his body. He didn't
let me go for one instant.

I would say I was discombobulated, but it's not a lovely enough word to describe the sensation. Disoriented, I think, deeply and dazzlingly disoriented. Dazed even. When the song ended, he let his hand run up my back to my neck for a second. I shivered. I broke away from his gaze finally, but it meant nothing by then, because he was already guiding me back to my table. He left wordlessly, without even a smile. And I sank into my chair. Clare and Connor were on the dance floor again, but Marie was there. I tried to smile, no big deal, but all she said was, "He looked pretty cool."

"Way," I said.

"Mysterious stranger," she said dreamily: then, more sensibly, "As they say, sometimes you just gotta dance."

"I guess," I managed to reply.

For the rest of the evening, no one could get me back on that dance floor. I was still stupefied, emotionally paralyzed. But I didn't want to replace that feeling with anything else.

# 22

## Sam

"Why did I pay good money for a Medico lock?" Grace asked, not unreasonably.

"A sound investment," I assured her.

It was a week since we had danced. She had opened her eyes, and there I was. I stood over her as she lay in bed with the covers pulled up around her neck. Then, what possessed me? I threw myself on the bed next to her, on the inside, near the wall. I was lying beside her on top of the blanket. She just looked at me with wide eyes and a little pulling-back gesture. It was well done, but it was not her.

"Wipe that innocent look off your face," I ordered.

She looked at the ceiling as if at an audience and shook her head a couple of times.

"Geez," she murmured, "God, what was I thinking? Whoa. Sorry about that. GET THE FUCK OFF MY BED," she shouted in a complete change of tone.

"Please," I said, ignoring her. "It is understandable where you got the notion, but it does not have to be the way you think it ought to be." I drew the stereotypical picture for her. "We meet in some low-key way, in the course of your job, say. Perhaps we arrange to have lunch, next time, dinner, the first kiss, which gradually builds, and then after we have become better acquainted, we make the gentle move into the bedroom. It can simply happen like this—because you want me and I very much want you. Without the preamble. Which we are well beyond now."

"And you'll still respect me in the morning? And someday you'll surprise me with that engagement ring?" she asked sarcastically.

"They are not in—, in— Damn, what is the word?" I looked around, at a loss.

"Oh, I know what you mean, in— Do you ever have that happen? Where you catch someone else's inability to think of a word? You know exactly what they mean and the word just disappears from you the way it disappears from the other guy?"

We lay thinking about it for a moment.

"Incompatible. Mutually exclusive," she said in triumph.

" 'Mutually exclusive,' " I repeated. "They are not. . . . I know what your problem is."

"I know what my problem is. What do you *think* my problem is?"

"You think there is something wrong with wanting sex—plain and simple."

"Plain and simple," she said, then nothing.

"It would be rather charming, if it were not confusing you a bit. And ruining the evening."

Nothing.

"I must say, you are not the kind of woman with whom I typically become involved. Usually, these are women who 'deal the sex card,' as a friend of mine once put it, right off the top of the deck. No qualms for them at all. You seem to think I would prefer a virgin."

"Gee, and I thought we were talking about me," she muttered. "Guess what? I don't want to play cards. I want to date. I want to stare across the table at someone who's looking me back deeply in the eyes. Holding my hand across the table. Or under it," she added.

"And I would not want to do that if you jumped on me now, correct?"

She jumped on top of me. "Hey, Sam," she

said in a mean voice. "Since we're being so honest"—she made the word seem like a curse—"with each other, what's your real name?" she whispered roughly.

I could not speak for a moment. "Aleksandr. Aleksandr Galynin." I tried to say it easily, and, as usual, with no accent, but I may not have been able to keep my face a blank.

"That's just great. My Comrade Right," she uttered dolefully.

"Former comrade. So let us do something to take your mind off of the ugly truth," I suggested. "Off of many ugly truths."

"You'd like that, wouldn't you? But I have to think."

"Do not think."

"But I have to think about whether not to think."

"Not really." I took her left hand from my shoulder, where it was supporting her as she crouched on top of me. She had apparently forgotten to move away after her interrogation. I kissed her hand. She did not pull it away. "Maybe you will be surprised. Maybe I will still respect you in the morning."

"Maybe you'll be surprised. And you'll damn well respect me more in the morning. And don't presume to think you understand me."

"That is the spirit," I said encouragingly, pulling her down on top of me.

I could see her mouth start to form words. I think they were *Wait a minute*, but they never left her lips. I felt a thrill as she began to respond to my touch. I could hear the little sounds she made now with my own ears, firsthand. I kissed her tenderly on the lips, on the edges of the lips, all over her face. She moaned into my mouth. She kept her eyes closed. When I moved to her neck—the skin so delicate, I feared I would leave marks—her body arched toward me and then away. I moved my hands along her side, lightly at first, and she started wiggling. I fondled a birthmark on her hip. Moving my mouth to her shoulders, my hands found their way to her breasts. She nearly broke my teeth with her collarbone as she writhed in response. She was very sensitive there. The more lightly I stroked them, the more vivid was her reaction. I had to taste them, though apparently I was taking my life in my hands. Her sounds were something approaching a purr. One second, she held me close as I teased her; at another, she would try to push me away. With my tongue, I continued to explore other places—her belly, her arms, her back, her sides—but I had to return again and again to her breasts just to experience

that response. Although even when I kissed
her a few inches above her hip on one side,
she kicked out wildly. I think I may say that
she seemed very excited.

She became uncharacteristically still as I
moved down below her hips; she knew what
was coming next. A little fearful of my physical safety, I moved my head between her
legs after nipping a bit at her inner thighs.
Her body became quieter now, although her
breathing was ragged and loud. I tasted her,
diving deep with my tongue. Her hips
moved the most when I flicked her clitoris
gently, but I could not help sampling the
nearby areas as well. I am a born experi-
menter. I wanted to go on in this way for a
long time, but I had the impression she
would not last through much more. I may
have lingered too long. With several deep,
deep groans, she came. Her wiggling slowed
but did not stop. I pulled off my shirt and
slacks, stopping to fish a condom out of one
of my pockets, placed there earlier in anticipation, if not certainty.

As she lay panting, I quickly put it on, then
gently began to guide myself into her. Now
again I could look at her face, eyes closed,
one lip a little bitten. I was raised up above
her, and she put her hands on my shoulders.
She was tight but not unwilling, so I slowly
increased my thrusts, controlling for as long

as I could. But watching her from this close distance, I lost what composure I had left and found myself pushing almost roughly into her. She cried out, over and over. With every thrust, she seemed to catch her breath and let out something between a groan and a sobbing noise. I think I had in my mind some nonspecific theory involving varying our positions, but that would have to wait for another opportunity. I could not bear the thought of stopping this for a second. I delayed as long as I could, but after a few minutes I let release wash over me. I lay on top of her for a brief time. She was covered in sweat from my efforts. She stroked my back, seemingly without thinking. I kissed her face along the softly cut jawline. Now she had one hand over her eyes. I hoped dearly that what she was feeling was not regret. I wanted still more, but I could not bring myself to pull out of her quite yet. I knew that at some point I would have to, however, and so, rolling onto my side next to her, I broke the connection. Temporarily.

She lay without speaking, catching her breath for a while, and not looking at me. I said nothing, allowing her to relax into sleep. I lay and thought for some time. But after a couple of hours, I began on her again. This time, she grabbed onto me. Throughout, she tasted and touched me when I let her. This time, I approached her from many different angles. I will never forget her expression one time when she reached orgasm, her eyes reflecting back my own, I inside her—and the look on her face immediately afterward, as if coming back to her senses, almost startled to realize where she had just been, what had just happened. I did not leave her until very early in the morning. For a change, I wanted nothing more than to wake up next to the woman I had taken to bed. But that would have to wait.

I silently dressed and left her apartment as she slept, locking the door behind me. I used the lock pick a very different man had used to enter.

# 23

## Grace

David had been my safety school. Because I had him, I wasn't pressured by sex to get involved with someone. That's the wrong reason. And I knew him, liked him, and trusted him. He was a buddy. And while for me the sex was tinged with naughtiness, without which so little is worth doing, over time that special little charge faded. If you're having sex without love, I theorize, then there's got to be something beyond quality to keep it exciting. Novelty of some sort, maybe. I don't know. I know that as I wanted it less and less, that was enough to keep him inspired. But for me, unless we started some serious S-M or something, the amount of excitement that I could generate for the act was dwindling.

But even when I was thrilled to be having sex with him, he almost never stayed the night. That was my doing really. The last time he did, I had an allergic reaction.

We had fooled around late into the evening after watching a couple of late-night sitcoms, which we loved to do together (sometimes just over the phone). And afterward, he fell asleep, with his hand resting heavily on my thigh. He fell asleep. I lay there. I started to feel strange. Antsy. I felt crowded. As if I were going to jump out of my skin. I felt like a prisoner. Why does he still have to be here? I thought miserably. Why won't he go? Leave me alone.

That's when I concluded that I am an opposite polarity. Like those magnets. When one comes close to me—physically, not emotionally—I have to jump back on a little tuft of air.

I slipped out of bed and curled up on my couch. I felt much better. But he must have awoken a little. He reached out for me, and I wasn't there. So he lifted his head and spotted me on the couch.

"What are you doing?" he called out quietly, puzzled.

"I couldn't sleep. What's the matter?"

"Are you really gonna sleep there?" he asked.

"I kind of want to. Why?"

"It's creepy." He sounded a little hurt. "You're going to stay over there?"

"Go to sleep, honey. You won't even notice."

"Don't 'honey' me," he yawned. I heard a little more muttering, but then he quieted down. And left me in peace. But by mutual agreement, he didn't stay over again. He pleaded to, sometimes. He believed that I should not have a problem sleeping with someone else in the bed. I didn't say it was him. I don't think that it was. As things have worked out in my life, it's relatively rare for the people that I sleep with to stay overnight. That sort of thing happens more often with serious couples, which I am not (half of one). I don't always have this reaction. On some occasions, one simply passes out, and it doesn't matter who's there. But it's happened more than a few times.

I'm a lot like a man, I think. I like to fall right asleep after I've gotten mine. I like to read at the table. I don't like to feel trapped.

David thinks I just don't drink enough.

The loveliest thing Sam did for me that night when he did so many lovely things was not to be there in the morning.

# 24

## Sam

"Who the hell am I?" she asked.

"What a question," I laughed.

"I'm a different person when I'm with you."

"I do not think so," I said.

"Very funny. And how would you know?"

We were at a little corner diner near her home. I actually thought passingly of what an excellent location her neighborhood was for someone like me to live—nobody I knew would ever consider living there or even passing through, yet it was not such a dangerous area when you were in it. But as in most poorer neighborhoods, the grocery stores left a lot to be desired.

It was the night of the following day, so to speak. While I did not want to burden her with a confusing, alien presence that morning, I had stopped by her place that evening to check on her status—that is, to look at her again, in person.

I found myself truly enjoying being with her, even when she was irritable, as she was then. Perhaps especially when she was irritable—much more of her personality came out. And she seemed to like to try to irritate me.

She was working on a chocolate ice cream soda. I was nursing a scotch. One of her hands was holding her glass; I reached across the table and took it in mine. She pulled it away.

"I thought that is what you wanted," I said softly.

"Jesus, I don't know what I want. What are you doing with me?"

"Just lucky, I suppose."

"I don't have that kind of luck. I mean, I don't have standard good luck."

"You have managed to get away clean with three murders," I said very quietly.

"Not entirely clean," she said, looking up at me from her favorite spot, the table.

"Now, why would you want to hurt my feelings?" I asked.

That is when she laughed. I thought how lovely it was to sit there, teasing her and being laughed at. Very few people have ever done that to me. But when the right person does, you know. And she knew, as well; she just did not like it.

"Why do I act this way with you?"

"It seems to me you are just being yourself."

"Well, I'm sorry, but if I start to care about your feelings, I won't be. I never am."

"Then do not give a thought to my feelings. I seldom do," I said.

"This is too weird."

"Nonsense. This is simply what you would term *chemistry*," I assured her, ignoring a trail of dead bodies, her work and mine, that bound us together, in my humble opinion, more solidly than any random set of pheromones.

"Why aren't you more shaken up by this? You're clearly the stone-killer type, calm and collected and 'I work alone.'"

"Where do you get those expressions?"

"I watch a lot of movies."

I paused. "I am . . . shaken. But if there is one thing I have learned how to do, it is to improvise. And accept good luck when it comes my way."

She took a long breath. "I can't sleep with you again."

"Why is that?"

"I have to think. I have to figure this out."

"Ah, yes, thinking. You seem to set great

store by that, as I recall. But you are better when you forgo it." I meant that, by the way; it was not just desperation.

"I once knew some people who would disagree with you on that," she said. Then she blurted out, "Am I free, or are you gonna blackmail me?"

"Do not be absurd. Is that what you think I have done?"

"I think you took advantage of a situation," she said, again not looking at me.

"That is what I do. But you are not looking beneath my surface here. If you knew me better, you would realize . . ." Realize what? My God. "You would realize that this situation has taken advantage of me."

"Well, maybe I should get to know you a little better," she said slowly, finally looking up.

"Well, why not?"

"I'm afraid."

"I will not hurt you."

She rolled her eyes and noisily slurped the remaining traces of her soda from the bottom of the glass with her straw. "Maybe I'm afraid for you."

"I am actually pretty tough, not at all like my deceptively delicate appearance."

"What?" She looked at me, puzzled.

"Oh, sorry, not me. I must have meant you."

She pursed her lips a little in thought.

"I can take no for an answer, if that is what you want," I said seriously.

"I don't know," she whined.

"Well, shall we just find out, then?"

A minute or two of silent whining preceded her decision. "Okay . . . but no sex." Damn. And allow me to recapitulate. Damn.

"You are the boss," I smiled.

A little tentatively, she put her hand, frosty-cold from the soda, across the table. I took it. And we just sat there together for a while, not saying anything.

# 25

## Grace

So we started to date. We went to see *Cats*, and I loved it. Really. Also *The Phantom of the Opera.* Then Sam insisted on going to the real opera, thinking I would rebel. But I didn't. It was fantastic. We saw *Dido and Aeneas* at Lincoln Center. I got to dress up, and he wore a tux—just for the hell of it.

As we left the building after the show, we decided to walk a bit in the night before getting in his car. It was crisp out, but I didn't care. There's magic in opera, there really is. It's so larger than life and spectacular, literally. He asked me what I was thinking, so I told him. It was a rhyme I knew from childhood, when I used to read *Bullfinch's Mythology* over and over. "I'm not sure if I remember it exactly," I warned, "but pretty close." Then I recited it:

> *"Unhappy Dido was thy fate,*
> *In first and second married state.*
> *Thy flight the first one caused by dying.*
> *Thy death the second caused by flying."*

We walked a little more.

"Amazing," Sam said. "I am unfamiliar with that one."

"See, you don't know everything."

"I never said I did."

"It's implied," I said.

"Why do you think that poem stayed with you for so long?" he asked.

"Do you mean does it have special meaning to me? I don't know," I tried to answer my own question. "Maybe it does, when you think about it."

"Now let us analyze. Would I be the one whose death results in your flight?"

"No," I said very quickly. "I was thinking of you as the second, possibly. . . . If I grow too attached to you."

"Then who was the first?"

I didn't answer. I just walked on, and he seemed to forget after a few minutes. We found the car eventually, and he began the drive back downtown. I kept stealing glances at him as he watched the road. It was quiet;

we didn't have the radio on because, really, after opera, what's the point?

He looked a very cool customer. His face had quite a few lines in it. I've always liked that. It's not cool to admit it, but I grew up on Clint Eastwood and Charles Bronson, men who hid their feelings behind squinting eyes and chiseled faces, and I've always loved that look. Sam's weren't age lines so much as character markings. His dark eyes were fairly deep-set, and his nose was, well, I think you'd call it aristocratic. He was straight and tall, a little on the thin side. I could visualize his bare chest as I sat there, the ropy muscles in his arms, his lean form on top of me. I stopped myself because it was a bad idea.

I watched him drive. He did it well and a tad on the impatient side. He drove a stick. Of course. He moved pretty damn decisively in traffic, and it was when he was executing some complicated maneuver that I would get a glimpse of the side of him I only saw openly that horrible night with Ben. A sort of naked, unapologetic ruthlessness. Sometimes I saw him look around that way in a crowd. Hyperaware, coldly, competently vigilant. Not nice.

He was very controlled in aspect, like me in a crisis, only all the time. There was a certain authority to his movements, and an

economy. No wasted motion. And he didn't
walk like an American. There is a difference.
I'm sort of a connoisseur of walks. My first
and only boyfriend was a European; he
didn't carry himself like a carefree, leaden-
footed American boy. He almost danced,
touching down lightly with his feet, sort of
smoothly gliding. Sam walked more certainly than that, but not heavily, not glumly,
not casually. Dignified. Unconsciously conscious of himself. Not theatrical, not self-
effacing. Just confident.

It seemed to match his European background. I got a sort of old-world impression
from him; he carried European civilization
with him in this land of barbarians. That sort
of thing. Except sometimes when he spoke to
me, it was with a bluntness I've always asso-
ciated with us, not them.

He was very much a gentleman (except
possibly in his line of work, of which I still
knew little but suspected much). One of my
colleagues at the magazine was a boy from
the South; that's how I recognized it. He let
other people go first. He held doors and
chairs for me. When we arrived at my apartment that night, he turned off the motor and
got out of his side of the car, then came
around to mine to let me out. Normally, he
wouldn't have gotten the chance, but I was
still lost in thought.

He walked me through the outside doors—he let me unlock them, so I didn't see how he had broken in on earlier occasions—and then saw me to the door of my apartment. He wasn't making this easy. But he just took my hand and kissed it—appropriate, given how we were dressed—and said good night, looking at me seriously even though his mouth was smiling.

"Thank you for coming out with me tonight," he said. "Would you happen to be free on Friday?"

"Yes, I guess so," I muttered.

"Perhaps you would consider going dancing?" he asked with a grin.

"I don't think so. Not a good idea." He had to be kidding.

"Someday I will insist upon it." He shrugged his shoulders. "For the time being, we can watch others. The ballet. Better?"

"Much."

"I should be hurt."

"No, you shouldn't be. You know why."

He grinned again and blew me a kiss as he walked away down the hall. My breathing began to slow down a bit. He's good, I thought. I may be kind of an idiot, but I knew he wanted to sleep with me again. I really wanted to, too.

So why wasn't I? Only fear can overpower electricity. It killed me to feel him so near me.

When he touched me, I got that electric sensation I remember having when I was sixteen with my first and only boyfriend. I remember lying on a sofa with my head in his lap. He was stroking my hair, and I felt every single strand that he touched. When we kissed, just kissed, I felt it all through my body. Sam was like that, something I thought I'd never feel again. My breath speeded up when he was near, sometimes when he just looked at me. I felt completely taken, out of control, that night when we had sex. Every time he'd touched me, I'd felt a charge flowing through. God, he literally made me quiver that night, and shake, and . . . I don't want this! I mean, I do and I don't. Nothing feels like this. Nothing feels as good as this, feeling revved up just by someone's raw nearness to me. His physicality overwhelmed me that night. His breathing, his arms, his hands—they all felt so much bigger than me.

Stop it. Be sensible, Grace, he's not perfect. He's far from perfect. In fact, there's something really, really wrong with him.

But there is with me, too. It's not like I can forget that. Would he be so interested in me if I hadn't killed three men? Well, actually, since I've yet to determine how he found out about me in the first place, I can't know the answer to that. See? That's so like me. The danger is that all I'll think about is what he thinks of me. But what do I think of him? Huh, how about that?

He's a mystery to me, as I must be to him. I'm more than a little afraid of the solution. I have a feeling this is going to be a very grown-up version of "I'll show you mine if you show me yours." Neither one of us bears close examination.

# 26

## Sam

I was given the necessary information, per the usual arrangement: the target's name, age, occupation, residence, habits, acquaintances. Country: Argentina. Objective: elimination, while communicating a threat to the target's colleagues.

I could not allow my feelings for Grace to interfere with my work; to prove this, I had accepted the assignment. But, unfortunately, feelings are not quite so easy to control as I would have wished.

It was not just that when I thought of Buenos Aires, I visualized the pleasures that I could share with her there, the food, the nightclubs, trips outside the city. I wanted to teach her to dance the tango; I was sure I could talk her into it.

That was natural. What was less natural was that I was more curious than usual about the target. Perhaps it was understandable. It was a woman, about the same age as Grace, a reporter, although she was operating in the journalistic jungle of political and financial dealings in Latin America. She would not be the first to die for that. Apparently she had successfully gotten the goods on a corrupt politician. Sometimes I wonder why they try. Why they never stop trying. Her death will clearly be a murder, and the obvious lessons will be drawn. Yet I could predict with near certainty that the particular politico behind it would someday be caught in his own web. But enough philosophy.

My employer would have hired one of his local boys but, to achieve maximum psychological impact, this hit was to take place within the well-secured confines of the woman's newspaper office. Nervous at the rising toll the Fourth Estate was paying in the region, the newspaper had invested in a high-tech security system, replete with alarms, voiceprint and smart-card identification, bulletproof glass, the works. I could not walk in and shoot her, not because of the security—I was sure I could outwit that, if

need be—but because no identifiable individual was to be connected with the killing.
Death was to come—solely to her—almost as
if from God, not man: from outside this bas-
tion into the very heart of the news-gathering
machine, with no obvious middleman.

A very pretty problem.

Yet for the first time, perhaps not unpre-
dictably, I was experiencing qualms.

It was not impossible to see through the
bulletproof windows—I could watch her at
her desk from a convenient distance, a room
in a building across the street. Nobody
thinks of everything. All I had needed was a
plan of the pressroom, a decent gun, a basic
understanding of geometry and physics, and
a cell phone.

And a heart of stone, of course. The kind I
used to have.

Sitting in her chair at her desk, her heart
was approximately 3 feet from the floor.
Through one of the windows in the office I
had rented across from the press building, I
could see the target clearly. That was not the
window I would use, however. It would take
several rounds to break through the protective glass, if that, and the outcome would be
messy, not sharp. But the building that
housed the little opposition paper was a
fairly typical substandard construction of
concrete and steel. I would need a powerful

rifle, armor-piercing rounds, and a little experimentation time in the field—an actual field, that is. I would shoot her through the wall. My only handicap was that I would not be able to see her. I would have to know where she was. That was what the cell phone was for. I observed her work pattern for a few days. Then, having done the calculations both as to where she was in relation to the wall and the likely amount of deflection the bullet would experience on its path, I would call her up and get her talking. That way, I would know she was at her desk, where I wanted her to be. The second after she hung up, she would be dead.

The semiautomatic rifle I had chosen could drop an elephant in its tracks. The bullets were .50-caliber. I should only need one.

With the heavy gun balanced on its tripod, sticking almost invisibly out of the open window, I sighted not on the target but on where the target would be. I picked up the mobile phone and then set it down beside me on the floor. I sat back and began to think.

I had told Grace I would be out of town for the week, "on business." She had not asked any questions. And I had not volunteered any answers. She did not yet need to know.

So why was I doing this? I did not need the money, not from this job. It was a dirty one. Dirtier than most, I hasten to correct. I had not known what kind of target it would be before I had signed on for this one. I had worked for this particular employer before; he was reliable and discreet, if distasteful. But I had agreed. A deal is a deal, especially in this business. Once you get a reputation for not fulfilling a contract, the work really does dry up. Of course, I could tell him that it was impossible to make the kill under the limitations he had given me. But he knew my work; he would know it was not true. And, frankly, that was something my pride would not allow.

I grabbed another scope and moved to the window that mirrored hers. I took another look at her. It was strange—she did remind me of Grace. But that was pathetic. What if she had been a man? A big burly man who knew very well what he was getting into? But she was not.

Well, what were my options? I could leave the message that the job was completed and get the hell out of town. Not an ideal solution. I wanted to be able to return to Argentina someday. And I wanted to continue breathing. I could pass the word that the job was undoable. Except that if I made the decision not to kill this girl, I did not want somebody else doing it, and quite possibly making a mess of it—and her. Or I could do the job that I was trained to do. Do it, knowing that if I did not, somebody else would. And that if I stopped here, if I started exercising my own personal judgment in the matter, I was finished. Was that a good thing? I was who I was. Who was I to think I could or even should change?

I knelt in front of the rifle and sighted in again. I picked up the phone. I dialed the number. The reporter answered.

Damn. I believed that I had thought of everything. It was not the first time that it had been necessary to speak to a victim. It had never made the slightest impression on me. I silently debated what I should do. The assignment was not yet blown. I could call again, if I needed to. I pressed the disconnect button as her voice came over the line.

This was incredible. This was disastrous. What in God's name was I doing?

I sat immobilized for a minute. Then I wiped my eyes and proceeded to disassemble my equipment.

But it is not any easier to stop killing than it is to start. Before I left the country, I had to quietly ice the politico who hired me. Just to keep my future options open.

# 27

## Grace

He had to go away for a few days. Work. I don't know what that is.

Does he think about me when I'm not with him? God, there I go again.

# 28

## Sam

Back in town, I watch Grace as she sits beside me at the theater or a concert; she makes me feel both old and world-weary, and yet younger, rejuvenated. I find myself recalling some facial expression or gesture of hers as I read or cook or putter around the house, experimenting with new weapons. I have no plans to accept any more assignments for the moment. I will stay here for a while and see this through.

I would love to have her up for a meal, but I know the evening would end in the bedroom, and I want to respect her feelings in this matter, for as long as I can.

She remains very cagey with me. She cannot help noticing that I say nothing about my own past. I have not given up on the effort, but to really break through, I might have to reveal much more of myself than I ever have to anyone before. And quite frankly, I cannot yet conclude that that is such a splendid idea. The last thing I want to do is frighten her away. I like her. But could she like me if she knew what I am? Yet, to fall back on psychology, it seems possible that the reason we are together in even the limited fashion that we are is that there is potentially real honesty between us. When I remind myself that she is a killer, it does not distance me from her, but gives me the sense that perhaps she can eventually understand and, dare I say, love me.

I still do not know why she did what she did, but as a result, she straddles two worlds: one of relative innocence, where death is accidental and guilts are minor, and my world, where death is a means and sometimes an end and guilt is monumental. Generally, it is a mistake for someone like me even to remind himself that that other world exists, but I do not find it so distressing when I see it through her. And perhaps I can guide her over the divide, not into my world, but into a special one of her own, where, if she can learn to keep her balance, she can avoid falling into the abyss on one side or looking back with intolerable longing at the one to which she no longer belongs.

I have always considered myself an intellectual with an unusually broad arsenal, or rather, an intelligent, classically minded assassin, but I wonder if I am qualified for this task. I want to be. I would never have even considered it before. From a plateau built fairly firmly on artfully constructed rationalization, I, too, stand on a precipice. I do not know what she will cost me, this girl, but until now, the price exacted for what I have done has been too easy for me to pay. In my line of work, the plateau does not remain immobile; it gently, slowly descends into a land of utter soullessness. She has soul to spare. It may have to be my only religion at this late date.

I am forty-six years old. She may already have saved me from that dark and inconsolably lonely place. The least I can do is to try to return the favor.

# 29

## Grace

New York can be a dangerous place. I'm reminded of that fact every now and then. Marie and I were headed one fine afternoon to an early movie. For some crazy reason, we decided to walk. Maybe because it was a beautiful warm day and we wanted to enjoy it. Some dumb-ass thing like that. And so we set off. We were headed to the Angelika movie theater, which shows semi-independent movies, and even though I am morally opposed to theaters that are designed with the aisle down the middle of the room and the seats on the edge, this is often the only place that shows certain pretentious films we'd like to see.

Walking down a major though fairly

pedestrian-free street, innocently chatting—
that was us.

"I promise," Marie solemnly vowed. "I
will not drag you to another Andy Garcia
movie. I can barely force myself at this
point."

"I know you love him madly. I like him,
too. He's a babe."

"But if he's in a movie, it's almost certainly
a bad one," she finished.

"It's like Sam Neill," I added tragically.

"All right, all right, all right. Please don't
bring up *Dead Calm*."

"In over his head. Drowning in pre-
dictable plot devices. Oceans away from a
good film."

"Stop it," Marie implored, but she was
chuckling.

"At sea." I couldn't help it.

"Although everyone else thinks that was a
good movie."

"The decline and fall of Western civilization," I explained.

And then New York reality broke in. It so
often does. Marie walks around the city far
more than I do—to her job in midtown, to
her gym, to bars. She's black and she's
shapely. She gets a lot of attention, almost all
of it the unwelcome kind. Often she wears a
Walkman headset (my theory is that we
should wear them, but have the sound

turned off so we know what guys are saying, in case it's anything really threatening, but they will think we have no clue). Her reactions vary wildly: Sometimes she just ignores the random "Hey, baby," or "Ooh mama," or "Good-lookin'," or "Like that ass," or "Get me some of that"; sometimes she doesn't.

One night, some guy was harassing her from across the street and she started gesturing unpleasantly back at him, her fist raised, and asking him, "You want some? Huh, you want some? Come on and get it." She had been drinking a bit. Sometimes that can make you forget that you're not supposed to be walking down the street unworried and free-spirited. Friends of hers in a passing cab stopped and tried to hustle her away. Once, a boy on a bicycle pinched her butt as he rode by, obviously thinking he would get away with it easily. Umbrella flapping in front of her, she took off after him and basically ran him to ground, where, fortuitously enough, two cops, who thought he'd stolen her purse, grabbed him and shoved him up against a wall. The presence of law and order did nothing to elevate Marie's choice of words in that situation as she royally cursed the guy out, taunting him that he thought he'd get away with it.

But most of the time, aside from a few vulgar epithets, Marie does nothing, because

usually she's mistress of herself enough to
know that there are maniacs out there who
will kill you.

- I, of course, simply don't hear the things
guys say. I don't hear 'em; I don't see 'em.
That's the way we do things here.

But it still rankles. And I guess it builds.

So we were walking happily down the
street, gossiping about people we didn't
know, when a man we were about to pass
stopped us with a look. There's always that
moment when you don't know if you'll be
greeted by a legitimate request for directions
or something else. With this guy, it could
have gone either way. He wasn't dirty
enough to be homeless. Yet he wasn't
dressed for business. He could have been
anything. There was no way we could have
known what to expect. And, in a way, that's
the worst thing. Let's face it, we had each
seen our share of guys who made sexual
comments at us while we passed, and who,
when ignored, got nasty. You never get rec-
onciled to it, but you get used to it. With the
first "Hey, baby," you pretty much know
what will follow. But this wasn't like that. So
we gave him the benefit of the doubt.

In a language I'm not sure God himself
could decipher, the man said something to
us. We let him talk, then responded with
puzzled looks and a light "Sorry." We turned

and began to walk past him. And then from behind us, he snarled something; one of the words was *bitches.* It often is.

We walked on a few steps, but then . . . well, it was just one of those rare, unspoken moments. We looked at each other, Marie and I, and we both had the same thought: We had, for the space of a few innocent seconds, hoped for better.

And then we turned around in unison and began to beat the living shit out of him. It took only a few seconds. Together, we shoved him to the ground and began to kick at him with all our strength. There was nobody near enough to do anything, and nobody did. But we didn't even think of that. I was wearing my black cowboy boots with the pointy toes; Marie, her Doc Marten walking shoes. We kicked and we kicked and we kicked. Silently, except for a little grunting. His chest and back took the brunt of it, but I think his head got a little, and I personally got his knee at one point. When we turned, moments later, and walked very quickly away, the last thing I saw on his face as he writhed was agony. But that wasn't what was satisfying. It was the look he wore when we first knocked him down: pure, unvarnished shock.

We made tracks around a corner and down several small blocks before we stopped and looked each other over. Marie's jumper was a little askew, so I helped her straighten it out. With some old napkins from my backpack, I helped her wipe off her shoes. They were a little bloody. So were mine. We got all the spots we could see, and then we just stood for a moment. And smiled, a little breathlessly and wide-eyed. No words were necessary.

And then we made our way to the movie theater. Luckily for all concerned, it was a pretty civilized crowd.

# 30

## Sam

There was a spot of dried blood on her boot. I am quite familiar with the substance, in all of its manifestations. I was mildly perturbed. I had been holding the boot, turning it around in my hands almost absently, as I sat on the sofa, waiting for her to dress for dinner. The bedroom is not really separated from the living room in her apartment, so she does her changing in the one closet in the place, a large walk-in. She was at the far end of the rectangular space, in her bra, digging through a pile of blouses on a shelf, when I barged in. She jumped when I touched her shoulder with my finger. It is a good thing I had something else on my mind.

"Get out," she said, irritated. "You're not supposed to be here."

"What is this?" I asked, undeterred. She, the boot, and I were rather a tight fit. I could feel my heart begin to race.

"It's a boot," she answered, turning back to tall stacks of tops, as if to ignore me.

"Killed anyone lately?" I pursued.

"No."

"Walk through a crime scene?"

"No."

"Then what?"

"Hmmm, I'm not sure you have any need to know."

I laid my hand on her shoulder. She shivered.

"You see? You see? You're taking advantage again."

"I believe I am fully justified here. Let us not have secrets."

"Let's."

I let the boot fall and put my hands on her sides, standing right up against her. There was no place for her to back up. She just looked away, toward her sweaters. I placed my cheek against her hair. She put her hands flat against my chest as if to push me away, but she did not actually do it. I knew if she did not do it soon, it would be too late.

"My friend and I beat up a guy on the street who called us bitches."

I pulled my head back to look at her. "Out in the open?" I said aghast.

"Nobody paid any attention. We were gone a few seconds later."

My thumbs were creeping up toward her breasts. My hands had a mind of their own.

"He called you bitches?"

"Sure. It's not the first time I've heard that."

"That is all he did?"

"You don't have any idea what I'm talking about, do you?" She tried a little to pull away, but I held on. "He accosted us on the street, said something to us we didn't understand, and when we turned away, he called us bitches. We just snapped. He'll think twice next time."

"Was he a large man?"

"No, he was pretty short. Didn't matter to him. He never thought we'd actually do anything." She paused. "Hell, neither did we. Nine hundred and ninety-nine times, we don't."

I tsked a bit. "Then what did you do?" I was still concerned, although about what, I was not exactly sure. Possibly the future of mankind if women started to take men to task that way every day. But that would never happen.

"We disappeared. Don't worry about it. It

was kind of a beautiful moment. Please let go. I can't take this."

"Are you going to beat me up?" I was curious.

She kissed me instead, open-mouthed, letting herself fall against me, and, given the situation, that was worse. I was inches from fucking her right there and then. I let her go, because I knew if I did not, she would hate me later. I can still feel her at that moment. So close, so unbearably close. I backed out of the closet, kicking the boot behind me. I went to sit on the couch, trying to calm myself down. And I waited. She was some time in that closet. I wondered what she was doing.

To distract myself, I closed my eyes and tried to envision the sequence of events she had described. She was right. Women almost never do what she and her friend had done, even though, by rights, they should. Inveterately, men call out an unending series of remarks at women as they pass—sometimes warmly and appreciatively, sometimes roughly. I have seen it often without ever paying much attention. But the hostility underneath can be palpable—too many times, when these men are ignored, their follow-up comments are laced with anger. In an ideal world, even I have to admit, a woman would be able to punish such a man physically. But they almost never do. I had a colleague once, a woman with a well-earned reputation for viciousness in her work, who waited too long one night to recognize that a man following her down the street, loudly harassing her, was a real threat. We had all marveled about it at the time; she had been in a vacation spot, not on the job. She must have been in an off-duty mode in her mind, I realized now, just a typical female. The sound of heavy footsteps behind them must be a persistent sensation.

At dinner that night, Grace and I avoided discussion of the closet incident and focused instead on the male-female battle of the streets.

"You can't be on guard every moment," Grace explained. "We just try to pretend it's not happening, I think. Because most of the time, it's not. You know what I mean." She shook her head thoughtfully. "Sometimes I think—just to stay sane—we're trained not to believe the worst until we have to."

But unfortunately, it is not always possible to calibrate one's response with absolute accuracy.

# 31

## Grace

The man sitting to my right was beginning to get on my nerves. I had noticed him as soon as he sat down next to me at the bar. It was a tiny bar, and people were crowded up against one another, but it was right near my office, a convenient way station. I was lucky to have gotten the stool I was sitting on, and I had no intention of leaving it. But this guy was definitely tilting toward me, trying to catch my attention. He wasn't succeeding, so he moved on to more drastic measures. He spoke.

Now this was a mistake. There's almost nothing any man can say to a woman in a bar that she hasn't heard before, if not in life, then in the movies. It is a plumbed well.

"What's that you're drinking?" he began.

I looked at him skeptically. The thing is, I was a little distracted. I was wearing my cowboy boots, and I couldn't help thinking about when I'd last had them on. I find it really impossible, however, to snub someone completely.

"Alcohol."

"That looks like a pretty fancy drink."

"It is."

He paused. He wasn't quite sure what I was thinking. I was thinking that you have to be optimistic to the point of deep denial to come on to a woman at a bar. But that's me.

"Well, what is it?" he smiled ingratiatingly. "I might want to try it someday."

"It's a girlie drink."

"Oh, I'm comfortable enough in my masculinity," he said.

"It's a cosmopolitan. Vodka, cranberry juice, Rose's lime juice, and Cointreau."

"You don't mind drinking alone?"

"I prefer it."

"I don't believe that. You could be drinking that at home."

"It's a very sticky drink to make."

"My name's Ted."

"I'm waiting for someone, Ted."

"What's your name?"

"My name is legion, Ted."

"Seriously."

"I'm serious as a heart attack, Ted."

"Geez, what are you, a lesbian?" Ted had apparently arrived at this bar prelubricated.

"No, Ted. Just not interested."

"You know, I'm only trying to be friendly." Now, he had pasted a hangdog look on his face.

I cocked my head at him. "I know you are, Ted. But I'm afraid there's no future for us, Ted." I paused a moment and really looked at him. That felt a little strange. I almost never really look at them, but it wasn't so bad at all. I could see the little wrinkles around his eyes. I could see the tiny bit of flesh that was beginning to gather under his chin. He wasn't bad-looking. "You know, Ted, you're kinda cute. I'll bet you'll make some lucky girl a great one-night stand. But not me."

He raised his hands in a surrendering gesture, then leaned toward me one more time. "From your mouth to God's ear, babe." He turned away and started to scan the area for his next victim.

Sam materialized behind me. I had no idea how long he had been there. Not long enough, I thought.

"Are you going to finish that?" He gestured at my drink.

"I don't know. I usually don't."

He picked the drink up and tossed it down. "So I have noticed. Shall we dine?"

. "Lay on, Macduff."

"So sophisticated. Tell me, do you come here often?"

"What are you smiling at?"

"You. Did you know that you could be such a consummate bitch?" he asked, winking at me.

I decided to answer him seriously. "No." I didn't.

Sam just looked at me and smiled.

"Should I feel sorry for him? I feel sorry for him."

"No need. He has already forgotten about it," he reassured me.

"I don't know. Geez, I was really mean, wasn't I?" I asked as Sam steered me by the arm toward the exit.

"You must not backslide now. You did him a favor. If you had taken him home, he would be a dead man by morning."

I looked disapprovingly at him. By now, he should have known I don't appreciate that sort of joke. "Isn't there something in between?"

"Yes, but men in bars are incapable of receiving on that frequency. Particularly when they are bewitched by beautiful redheads."

I smiled and suddenly relaxed. Nothing terrible had happened. We'd both live, Ted and I. "You know, I should tell you something about that," I said, touching my hair.

"I have no need to know," he said, cutting me off. Taking my hand, he led me to his Jag, and a moment later we were on our way to dinner.

# 32

## Sam

She was early. She must have finished with her day's work sooner than she had predicted. This left her with extra time to sit in a bar, fending off potential suitors. I gathered this sort of interaction had been a trouble spot for her in the past. I must have arrived only shortly after she had, since I am habitually punctual. Her drink was only partially sipped, but really, that meant nothing; she is the slowest drinker in the world, and I am not someone given to hyperbole.

I noticed the man immediately. I recognized at first glance that he presented no threat to her, but would she? I stopped a little distance behind her, but neither one noticed me in the crowd.

I overheard the entire exchange. She was marvelous. She treated him almost the same way she treated me—no holding back. For a second, I might even have been a tiny bit envious. I quite prize our rather special relationship. But it can be only to the good if she learns to appreciate her own power. I did not want to have to interject myself in the situation, although I would have if she had shown signs of being overwhelmed.

She is definitely making strides. Still, I cannot always be around to protect her; I am thinking about giving her a gun.

# 33

## Grace

I often think, as I sit beside Sam at plays or concerts, that his appreciation of these things, the so-called finer things, seems like an essential part of his character. Self-contained, worldly—it is fitting that the old-fashioned pleasures are his preference. His Jaguar, his understated Euro designer suits, his self-possession—all match. I am the only thing that doesn't fit.

I don't mean outwardly. I'm no great beauty, but I clean up pretty good. Lots of men date significantly younger women, and he seems very middle to me, not old; fit, not decrepit. We don't look funny together or anything. I am just so not his type, except that, while I don't know exactly what he

does for a living, I have a good idea that it is
something shady. Not everyone knows how
to get rid of a dead body calmly, nor is it usually their first instinct on encountering one. I
am not about to forget that. But what is he
doing with me?

Until I know who he is, I can never figure
that out. All I know about is what I respond
to. He is someone who saw me first at my
worst. As a result, I've just never gotten into
the habit of covering up from him. But yet,
there is no "result" stage. From the first
moment, there just seemed to be an understanding. He calls it "chemistry." Maybe. To
me, he seems to be able to see me and know
me and not to be appalled. Not to judge. Or
else to judge from another set of standards
than most people. I'm not an ordinary person. I knew that before people started dying
around me. But it's kind of nice that he
doesn't hold that against me. Let's face it,
he's got to be a bad guy. No good guy could
like me. Not just because of what I've done—
as remarkably easy to live with as that has
proven to be—but because of who I am.
Whoever that is. Maybe he knows. People
always say that there's someone for everyone, but I never believed it.

But he, too, wants something from me.
Why am I not avoiding him? He leaves me be
most of the time. He's courtly, but not

oppressive. Why did I kill those boys? Oh, yeah, because I didn't like them around, and I didn't know how to break it to them. I didn't know how to leave them. I guess I just don't get the sense that Sam would be devastated if I turned him away. (The worst he would do, I think, is kill me. And I don't think he'd even do that. But he wouldn't try to make me feel bad.) Maybe because by every set of rules I've ever known, that's exactly what I should do. He's bad news. If he leaves me, I win. And if he stays, I . . . Maybe it's that he doesn't seem helpless and innocent, the way the first two guys did. He doesn't seem to need anybody psychologically. He doesn't remind me of me at all.

It's funny. I was nice to those guys, and they liked me. Which is how it's supposed to be, I guess, except if I'd stopped being nice, then they probably wouldn't have liked me. But I couldn't do it. I'm not nice to Sam, and he likes me anyway. He gets me, I guess. But how can someone so different get me so well? And what would happen if I decided I didn't want him around?

I think it was the Ravel that did it. We had gone to a concert, and the Frenchman was the featured composer. Frankly, *Bolero* is his weakest work; it's flashy, but everything else I heard was moving and transporting. My head was full of it by the end; I wanted to go to a quiet bar somewhere, but Sam insisted on a little spot in NoHo with continuous loud music, so loud and so unmusical, he argued, that it was almost as good as none at all.

Sam seemed moved as well after the concert, though perhaps a little strained. It's pretty hard to tell with him, but I thought I detected something. Maybe because I was looking at him harder than usual. He doesn't smoke nearly as much as I do, but he lit one up immediately.

"The *Pavane*," I yelled across the tiny table at him.

"Yes," he shouted back, looking up.

"That was kind of magical for me. I thought I recognized the name, *Pavane pour une Infante Défunte*. When I was a little girl, I read these wonderful books. They were each about a lonely preteen, and there was always something supernatural in the stories, something that enabled the kid to come to terms with whatever was bothering her. And one story had this girl in it who was a pianist, and she was in a house for the summer that was haunted by the ghost of a dead young Spanish princess, and the girl spent the summer working on getting that piece of music right and setting the dead girl's spirit at rest. It was a wonderful story, and I didn't know there really was a song like that."

"It is like that," Sam agreed.

"What gives?" I asked.

"Perhaps you can set my spirit at rest."

"Are you haunted?" I asked.

"I am a killer," he shouted, simply. There were tables on all sides of us. We were in a corner, sharing the banquette. Through the din, there was absolutely no chance anyone could hear us. I could only just hear. And anyway, this was New York.

"Who isn't?" I observed, being a bit flip, I admit.

"I am a professional killer," he said very clearly and distinctly. Again, I looked around, but no one had heard a thing. Everyone was shouting.

"Hmmm," I said. He was as nervous as I'd ever seen him—that is, barely perceptibly.

"I think it is only fair to tell you. That is what I do for a living."

What do you say? He chose well; it's not as if I was in a position to criticize.

"Did you just not know how to tell people good-bye?"

He laughed a little. "Ah, I know only too well how."

"Why?"

He looked at me.

"Are you ashamed?" I asked.

"Ashamed of not being ashamed. But less

with you than I would be with most people, I imagine."

"Let's not talk about me here. How long? For whom? Why? Still?"

"Since I was twenty-one. For my government. I have a gift. The last time was . . ." He paused for a moment, gazing away into space. "Sometime before we met. For the private sector now."

"What kind of gift?"

"I can always find a way. And I have no qualms."

"You know, I would have said that about you."

"You are the only civilian I have ever told."

"Gee, this gives new meaning to the joke 'I could tell you, but then I'd have to kill you.'"

"I will never hurt you." He saw my mouth begin to move. "Or kill you painlessly." He smiled a tiny bit.

"To what do I owe that honor?"

"Can you say the same to me?"

I frowned and looked down at the table.

"Not to worry," he said generously. "I will never give you the opportunity."

"No, no. I don't want you to think like that. To have to be on guard all the time. That would be too awful, to live like that."

"You tell me."

"You stop that. Don't you be understanding and analyzing me right now. We're talking about you. . . . Did you ever want to stop?"

"No. I never saw it as a problem. I never had any higher aspirations."

"God, this is like that movie, *The President's Analyst,* where the CIA agent tells his shrink that he kills people, and the shrink says, 'It's a sensational solution to the hostility problem.'"

"Show it to me."

"Mmm, it would be a major step in our relationship if I started forcing you to watch my favorite movies."

"Maybe I can look forward to that." Jesus, he sounded almost, well, wistful, if you can be wistful through major decibels.

"I don't know what to think," I said.

"There is no set response. Unless it is to run shrieking from the room. Which is what you probably should do. If you were to heed my advice."

"I'm not good at taking advice."

"For which, at this moment, I am eternally grateful."

"Why are you being so human?"

"I apologize. It is rather an awkward moment for me."

"That's better. Jesus."

"Maybe I should take you home."

I let him guide me out of the noise and into the quiet of his car. An assassin, huh? Hmm, is that how he always manages to find a parking space? It'd be one method. He walked me to my apartment door and then followed me in. I was putting my backpack away and taking off my shoes. 'Cause of the rug. He was lingering.

"Should I make some tea?" he asked.

"No. I'm fine."

"I would like to stay with you tonight."

"Gee, dare I say no?"

"This is something I never want you to joke about. Of course you may dare."

"I don't think we should have sex again yet," I said slowly. "I don't know how I feel."

"Then sex is out. We can merely sleep."

I looked at him with my eyebrows raised and a skeptical expression.

"I can if you can," he teased.

Geez. I didn't really want to kick him out. Actually, I wanted him to stay. As he drank his tea, I washed my face and changed into a T-shirt and boxer shorts, two actions that should certainly have kept his libido at bay. A little awkwardly, we crawled into bed, in matching outfits, as it turned out, although my boxers were prettier than his. I turned on my left side, away from him, and he, surprisingly naturally, curled his body around me—spooning, it's called.

We were both quiet for awhile, but neither of us was sleeping.

He must have noticed how tense my body was. How could he not?

"Do you not want me to be here?" he whispered.

"No."

He thought a moment, then muttered, "I know what I just asked. . . . Do you not want me to kiss you?"

"No."

He kissed the back of my head.

"What do you not want me to do?" he continued.

"The real eternal question: What don't women want?" I chuckled.

"I am actually happy just being here," he said straight out. "I see no reason why it ever has to end."

"No," I answered, "but I never do."

"But I might be your Comrade Right," he cooed into my ear.

"Former comrade," I murmured.

I consciously tried to relax. It was easier than I thought it would be. His arms were around me and his breath was on my neck. It was hard for me to believe the next morning, but it wasn't long before I fell deeply asleep.

# 34

## Sam

That night, I experienced something dangerously close to delirium. As I lay in the bed by her side, I felt safe. Oddly, I felt trust. I cannot think of a time when I have felt so comfortable, playing as little of a role as it is possible for me to play. I would never have thought I would willingly make myself so vulnerable in front of someone, but that is exactly what I have done. Grace now knows who and what I am, yet there she was, knowing that, and lying, relaxed, in my arms.

There is no coercion here, no double threat, no misunderstanding.

There is, in fact, the hitherto unimaginable possibility of understanding. I do not yet comprehend her by any means, but I feel a sense of responsibility toward her. And I have laid upon her something almost anyone else might consider a burden, but that she just might be able to accept.

While, at first, I thought her refusal to have sex with me was the result of my self-revelation and her consequent revulsion, it took only a few moments to conclude that it was something else entirely. She was not afraid of me, but of what I represent: the promise—or threat—of a genuine bond, something that, had I not been so absorbed in her reaction, I might reasonably have focused more on myself. Even curled up in my embrace, she was attempting to maintain her distance. I was literally holding a paradox in my hands.

Or is the more apt metaphor that of a hand grenade from which I had just removed the pin? Like any other man, I have no idea what the woman I love will do. But I have large reserves of patience; it is a prerequisite in my line of work. I can wait.

# 35

## Grace

It couldn't have been the food. It was top-line
stuff, fancy, French. Although if the man
across the table from me ate this way a lot, it
would explain his slight tubbiness. He was
interesting; I think what he had was
charisma. Not a lot, just enough. And that's a
funny thing, because he was not, by any
stretch of the imagination, handsome. He
had a round face and was seriously balding.
His fingers were a little stubby. But his eyes
were very alive, very powerful. I think that
happens when you make a ton of money. It
gives you something you wouldn't otherwise have. The man worked with an investment bank. There had been some talk of
constructing a series of newsletters on

emerging markets investing. We'd provide the journalists, and the bank would contribute the funding. I had been dispatched to begin talks over the direction such a newsletter would take.

He was one of those successful rich people who had an unrestrained curiosity about everything and everybody. That was their bread and butter. Or their baguette and garlic butter, as it happened to be that night. He quizzed me on my background in the business, where I'd gone to school, who my parents were, what they did, what articles I had written, where I had been in the world. Straightforwardly and concisely, he told me his own story. He was a self-made man, and, at forty-eight, still unmarried. He looked older than his age. We discussed the situations in Africa, Eastern Europe, and Latin America. I found that, when pressed, I couldn't help myself from describing my background, answering his questions. Maybe it was his eyes.

We were at this midtown restaurant for three and a half hours. I found myself growing strangely weaker over the course of it. At the beginning, I was parrying his impertinent inquiries fairly well. At some point, I did answer them. By the end, I was just listening to him hold forth, which he did in a firm, self-confident voice.

I was beginning to feel slightly nauseated,
but I didn't know why. He kept trying to
catch my eye, and I kept avoiding his glance.
I really hadn't had that much wine, although
he had insisted we try at least three different
kinds to match different portions of the meal.
He had begun to tell me about myself, but he
had me all wrong. He thought I was holding
myself back from life's great experiences. I
should travel more, sample more places,
more people. Not stay in a little cubicle in my
circumscribed portion of the city.

It was the undercurrent. I avoided identifying it for as long as I could, but as we
finally rose to leave, he took my elbow to
steer me to the coat check, and I didn't know
how to remove myself from his touch. I felt
so strange. He insisted on helping me with
my coat, and he kept a hand on my arm as
we exited the room. The air hit us as we
walked out, and I shivered for a moment. He
put a hand on each of my shoulders from
behind for just a few seconds, to warm me, I
guess. Then we started walking a bit down
Fifty-second Street. "You must come to my
hotel for a minute; I'll show you what I
mean," he said. "I brought back some amazing artifacts from Uganda that will make you
understand what you are missing." He lived
in the Hamptons, he explained, but had not
yet had a chance to stop there after his most

recent trip, and tomorrow he was headed to Washington. It was the oddest thing. I felt mindless. Overwhelmed somehow. On some level, I had known from shortly after this business dinner had begun that he had decided to sleep with me.

For some reason, I felt powerless. We were going to his hotel. I had, somehow, no say in the decision. Or I couldn't say no. My stomach was churning. He kept a hand on my arm, being gentlemanly, of course. I felt caught up in something, something old, unbeatable. Then we were crossing the street toward his hotel. A wave of something came over me, and I had to stop in front of a car parked on the street. The light was against us anyway. I put my hand to my stomach and started to say I wasn't feeling well. His face was a blur to me. He was leaning over me, trying to look into my eyes. A large truck was speeding down the road toward us. It was a very big truck. It was going to try to beat the light. I had only one chance. Bending toward me, he was not solidly planted on the concrete. I grabbed his upper arms; he looked at me, not displeased. The truck was bearing down on us. On him, if I just gave him that shove.

"No!" I said. I let go of his arms. I motioned him away. "I don't feel well," I said desperately. His face started to shift from disappointed to concerned. And he stepped back to give me some space.

Into the street. And the truck crushed this millionaire to death instantly. I turned away, screaming, and collapsed against the hood of the parked car.

There were people, lots of people, suddenly, where there had seemed to be no one before. Two women set me down carefully on the curb and patted me gently on the back. An ambulance and a police car arrived very quickly, it seemed. I was sobbing as a policeman tried to talk to me. Everyone assumed immediately it was an accident. I saw the truck driver talking, confusedly, to one of the cops. His eyes were as wide and uncomprehending as my own. It had occurred too fast for either of us to understand. He would never know what had happened. And at that moment, I wasn't too sure myself.

The policeman was able to get my name and phone number from me, but that was a major accomplishment, as I could barely speak. I just nodded as he speculated on the hideous event. It seemed forever until the body was scraped up off the street by the emergency medical people. By then, I was crying so uncontrollably that even the policeman was patting my arm, trying to console me. He asked me if I wanted to be taken to the hospital, but I shook my head no. I just wanted to go home, I said. And they were so nice that two of them drove me there as soon as they were able to leave the scene. I quieted down a bit in the cruiser as we drove. As we pulled up to my building, the men said that they had my number and name but that hopefully they wouldn't have to bother me. Everybody had seen what had happened. How could I explain what I had done? Or hadn't quite done? One of them gave me a card with a therapist's name on it for dealing with my trauma, if I needed it. The other one said I should have a good stiff drink when I got in.

When I closed the door to my apartment behind me, I just leaned against it for a few moments before taking the wiser officer's advice. Fifteen minutes after I got home, the phone started ringing. I knew who it was. I didn't answer. And I turned off my answering machine. After a few minutes, it rang again. I just let it. I didn't want to talk to him. Did he know? It would not have surprised me somehow. Finally, the ringing stopped. All I wanted to do was sleep. I curled up under the covers, still in my clothes, and checked out for a while.

# 36

## Sam

What in the hell had happened? Something was very wrong. She was out of control. Did I push her to this? Was I involving her in something too serious too quickly? Was it something about the man? I had thought she was moving beyond this.

I sat in my car across the street from her apartment, the cell phone useless in my hand. I did not really know what had happened between them. I had watched her enter the restaurant early in the evening. I knew it was a business dinner. I could not help myself—I was simply curious. I assumed they would be done in an hour or so. Over three hours later, they had still not come out, and I found myself wondering at her ability to talk politics apparently endlessly. I would have left, but by this point I had been there for such a length of time that I thought I might as well see the evening through. She did look a little somnambulistic as she walked down the street with him. I was too far behind them to see what then occurred, but I did not need to.

Why such backsliding? He could hardly have been any sort of threat. And he had certainly not looked irresistible. I sat for hours in the car that night. I was used to that. The light remained on through her window, but there was no sign of movement. I moved the car farther away from her door before dawn. Late in the morning, she left her building, looking wan and sad. She took a cab to her office. She stayed in at work all day, then went straight home.

She did not answer her phone for all of that week, at least not when I called. I only tried once a day. She left her answering machine on. Finally, on Friday, she picked up when I rang. She agreed to see me the next evening.

My state of suspended animation would be alleviated then, I hoped.

I missed her.

# 37

## Grace

I couldn't avoid Sam forever. That is, maybe I could, but I didn't know if I wanted to permanently. But I was feeling a little delicate, to say the least. I kept seeing that man just before he stepped away. Stepped away because I asked him to. What a farce. What a tragic farce. I didn't kill him, but I might as well have.

Well, I don't see why I have to explain anything to Sam at all, I thought. He doesn't even have to know. Of course, he might wonder what had been going on with me during the week, but then, they say it's good to keep a little mystery in a relationship.

We had a salad at a restaurant near the Lincoln Plaza Cinemas and caught a Bosnian film. You can't say that every night. I said I was tired, I'd been very tired all week, and that I wasn't up for anything more. He tut-tutted a bit, sympathetically, and obligingly drove to my home.

"It has been rather a wearying week for me, as well," he said as we pulled up.

"Places to go, people to kill." The words were out before I thought.

He moved his jaw around for a minute. "Hmm, was that my week or yours?" he asked tightly.

I jumped out of the car before he had a chance to come around to my side. But he got out anyway and followed me in.

"I said I was tired," I noted as he closed the door behind him.

"I know. It must be something going around."

What do other couples fight over? Money? Wait a minute—couples?

"I would like to sleep here tonight," he added.

"What if I don't want you to?"

"Say it."

But I wanted him there with me. "I'm just not up for a lot of conversation," I said instead, with my brow furrowed, beginning to pout.

He reached out and moved my lips into a smile, a striking gesture, coming from him.

Then he pulled me into his arms, against his chest, and just held me there for a minute. I didn't argue. He let me go and I started my nightly ablutions. When I came out of my tiny bathroom, he was lying on his back under the covers of my bed, his hands under his head. I turned off the overhead lights and sat on the edge in my oversized T-shirt.

"I have a confession to make," he said.

"Oh, Jesus. Should I turn on CNN? Is the President dead?"

"I think you will find it a bit more upsetting than that."

"Oh."

"I have been watching you."

"What do you mean?"

"When you have been unaware of it," he elaborated.

"Like a detective?" I asked.

He laughed a little to himself. "Like an assassin."

"For how long?" I wanted to know.

"Off and on, since you met that boy in the bar."

"What?" I'm sorry, but I couldn't believe my ears, hackneyed as that thought was. "Why?"

"That night? For no particular reason. You struck me as the most interesting woman in the place. I was testing out some eavesdropping equipment."

"Gee, I guess I'm lucky it wasn't a new weapon."

"I was attracted to you."

"Jesus."

He said nothing. "Ever since then," I said.

"Off and on, yes. As time went by, more on than off."

"Until this moment," I began, mimicking the guy in the Army-McCarthy hearings, "I had no idea how low—"

"This bothers you. I murder people for a living. You kill them in your spare time, but this is over the line."

"It's really sick," I said. "I mean, God. Did you use your listening devices on me?"

"Only until I knew you."

" 'Cause after that it would be rude."

"Yes. As a matter of fact. By my lights."

I had turned toward him on the bed. "I really don't know what to say. Should I be flattered or weirded out?"

"I think you are the perfect woman for me," he said quite seriously.

"Are you mad?" I half-shrieked. "You know what I've done. Everything, apparently. What happens if you keep leaving the toilet seat up?"

"I was not aware that I had," he muttered thoughtfully.

"Do you think you deserve to die for it? I mean I don't know what will make me do it next. You're obviously as disturbed as I am, but are you really willing to take that risk?"

He pulled me down to him on the bed and arranged me, spoonlike, in the crook of his body.

"I refuse to worry. All I know is that it is impossible to imagine ever getting tired of you."

"Well, that may be a commentary on the limitations of your imagination," I snapped back from within his embrace.

"You have a talent for self-deprecation."

"I thought I was getting us both there."

He was silent for a few moments. But I wasn't through.

"You know, I don't know. What kind of people are we? This could be a recipe for disaster."

"It might be if you have already fallen into cliché."

"Don't fucking joke." I pushed him away. "I know what you're capable of. And I have no idea what I'm capable of. We're monsters."

"Birds of a feather." He reached for me again, and I pushed him away again, harder. His head hit the bookshelf next to the bed, and he came toward me again—to do what, I didn't know. I stuck my forearm, elbow forward threateningly, right in front of his Adam's apple at the same time he wrapped his right hand around half my neck. His thumb was almost pressing on my windpipe.

"See? See?" I said breathlessly.

With his thumb, he started to caress my throat. His body untensed, and he gently moved the arm I was threatening him with up over my head. He lay his own, facedown, against my breast, which at that moment, I have to say, could only be described as heaving.

"I was not going to hurt you. I would never hurt you," he murmured into my chest.

Yeah, right, there was a second there, though . . .

"Get out. Now." I said firmly.

Astonishingly, he unwrapped himself from me and, untangling himself from the covers, started to climb over me and out of bed. I bit my lip. "Are you going?" I asked, stupefied.

"I believe so. That is what you want," he replied with no emotion.

"Really?" I asked.

He looked a little exasperated. Finally, I thought. "Just tell me what you want," he demanded quietly.

I looked at him. It wasn't a trick. He had picked up his pants. "Would you come back another time, ever, if I asked you to?"

He looked abashed and smiled mirthlessly, "Yes, I probably would."

"Then don't go," I said. "Please."

He raised his hands in the air, palms up, questioning.

"Stay."

He put his pants back down on the chair where they'd been. He stayed.

# 38

## Sam

She was in my arms again, a position to which I would have liked to have become accustomed. Although it was terribly difficult to keep her there sometimes.

After much back-and-forth discussion, which, at certain moments, made me nervous about our long-term prospects, she was settled in bed with me. I found myself unusually pensive as we lay together.

I could not stop myself from observing, "I have never been as angry as you."

"I'm not angry," she said, surprised.

"You are a very angry little person."

"I am not an angry person. And I am not little. I'm medium."

"Hello!"

"Stop that. That sounds ridiculous from a middle-aged Russian."

"Completely off the subject, my dear," I noted. She gave what she herself had previously called a small "ritz-and-fritzing" noise of irritation. "What then do you consider the motivation for your actions?"

"I can't bear to hurt anyone's feelings."

"You have no difficulty hurting my feelings," I pointed out.

"I guess your life's not in danger, then," she said.

"Oh, I guarantee it. But that is not the reason why."

"You think you know everything, don't you?" she said after a few seconds.

"No. I am asking you."

"Well, do you have to know everything tonight?"

"Not at all. There is plenty of time for that," I said.

She turned her head around toward where I was, behind her.

"That's about the most aphrodisiacal turn of phrase I've ever heard."

"Is that a word?"

She continued, ignoring my interruption. "It's the most flattering thing anyone has ever said to me." A pause. "The most

exciting." A longer pause. "And the scari-
est."

She turned back to her pillow. I just held
her close. I had not even thought about what
I was saying as I spoke. But as the old song
has it, I seconded that emotion.

# 39

## Grace

This is scary. I think he loves me. Or thinks he does. How can he? How can I? But I really like myself when I'm with him. Because he does, maybe. With every nasty thing I say. God, it's such a relief.

Except with my closest female friends, I'm so not that with anyone else. All my life, for varying reasons, I've tended to take the high road. To make people like me. To make them not hate me. I choke back my worst impulses. Well, actually, I don't even think them until too late. Everybody else has always been better at being mean than I am. At keeping me looking for their approval. I just didn't want to lose them. Since I was very little, being extra, extra considerate was

the best way. Their feelings counted more.
You stop even asking why. Okay, maybe I
wasn't just afraid of hurting their feelings,
those guys. Maybe, ultimately, I was afraid
of their hurting mine. Or their feelings were
mine. God, I don't know. Geez, it's bad
enough to do the things I've done without
trying to figure out why. Something. Something stopped me from simply saying what I
felt. However I might have hurt them, they
could always hurt me more.

But I've just stopped caring. Well, I hope I
have. As long as I can avoid caring, people
have a better chance of continuing to breathe
around me. If they're not unlucky, too, like
that millionaire guy. If only I had spoken
sooner.

Anyway, Sam likes me no matter what I
do. Or say. So, he's a conscienceless killer.
And apparently a voyeur. I'm not perfect
myself. You don't toss love back in just
because it's not big enough. Because the
other person has a few flaws. There aren't a
lot of fish in the sea like him. Or me.

# 40

## Sam

One night, not long after our latest tête-à-
tête, Grace and I went out to dinner (Italian)
and a play (inscrutable). Both were in her
neighborhood, which explained much but
not all. As we strolled along toward her
apartment, I was still reviewing in my head
everything that was wrong with the little
piece of experimental theater to which I had
subjected us. It was not entirely unreasonable that the leading man was a woman. But
the leading woman was a terrier. And the
Greek chorus was a heavy-metal band. How
long had I been out of New York?

On the Lower East Side, euphemistically
known as the East Village, it was possible to
observe many aspects of life that in other

neighborhoods more typically remained hidden from view. As we passed by a parked car along the way, we noticed inside it a middle-aged couple arguing vituperously. His voice was harsh, low, and intense. The woman was shrieking. They were both cursing viciously, in two languages. I glanced at Grace, expecting to share a superior smile, but she looked surprisingly uncomfortable.

"What is the matter?" I asked, naturally. Perhaps she was still cogitating on the play. Not that she had been quite herself since the latest death.

"It's funny. It just kind of took me back," she said after a few moments.

"Back where?" I felt I had to be careful here.

"Home," she said simply.

"Did your parents fight often?"

"That's all they did."

"Not like that."

"No. Worse. It's just so funny, because even though I saw that every day of my life, there's been nothing like that in my life for the last ten years. Whatever else has gone on, nothing like that. Mostly, I don't even remember it."

I said nothing. I wanted her to go on.

"The only times I ever really remember it are, occasionally, in dreams when I'm back there. And the tension is so thick, constant tension, not knowing at any moment what will set them off. And no way to escape."

"So you did not have a very happy childhood," I offered, somewhat inanely, I confess.

"Did I ever say I did? Did you?"

"Yes," I chuckled a bit. "As a matter of fact, I did."

She looked puzzled. "Everything is not easily explainable," I added. In answer to her unspoken question, I made the effort, even so. "I was always very inventive. And that talent eventually came to the attention of those who had many ideas as to how to utilize it. I did not start out killing. I was a planner, a strategist, but it eventually became apparent that I was the man most capable of carrying out my own ideas. . . . And it was war."

"Hmmm. That war is over," she noted.

"And I am still killing."

She said nothing. I changed the subject.

"So in your dreams, you can never escape."

"Well, I couldn't, could I? I was a kid. But I can't really remember the sensation except when I'm in the dream right then. But I know the tension was always there. And I did try to keep people calm. I don't know. I don't remember much."

She shook her head—to herself, really. Or perhaps not.

"Sometimes," I said, "you are a little hard to read."

"No," she said. "Sometimes I'm just gibberish. . . . Like that play." She smiled. The moment was over. I would get nothing more out of her. Nor she from me.

# 41

## Grace

Sam didn't follow me inside that night, and I was glad. He keeps pressing me. I don't want to describe my past.

I don't want to remember it. Death threats, violence, fighting, blah, blah, blah. I just want things to be civilized. Controlled. Quiet. That's all I've ever wanted. I stayed away from men (and my family) because of the potential for noise. Noisy emotions and noisy violence. Noise and confusion and people's feelings getting hurt. God, the only thing worse than the noise was the silence. When they would stop talking to me, have nothing to do with me; I had done something wrong, hadn't put them first. After a few days, I would have forgotten what it was I had even done to bring it on. And they would act as if I didn't exist. Until they got their way. That silence was even worse than the fighting.

I would never do that to anyone. And I will never let anyone do that to me again. Anything but that.

# 42

## Sam

For a moment, I was frozen, even though I should have expected it, given the neighborhood. I was walking down Fourteenth Street, heading toward her home on a late Saturday afternoon, when suddenly a swarm of police officers materialized directly in front of me. My first thought was that they had somehow found out about her. My second was to calculate, with the basic materials I always had on hand, how many of them I could disable. Then I saw several poor local specimens being handcuffed roughly and shoved against the walls of the buildings that lined the street: Marijuana dealers, I realized, were the targets here, not my girlfriend.

A great wave of relief washed over me.

How little they knew. My little flower, deadly as she is, seems uncomfortable with dissension. Uncomfortable with what happens when unstable humans come into close contact with one another. I can understand that. Perhaps her nerves were shattered at an early age and now she has no patience left. Endless patience, it seems, and then none. The world is not kind to young females. It places so many demands upon them. She simply does not seem to know how to turn down the volume of those demands. She only knows how to turn it off.

She would be happiest, I suppose, with some sort of calculating machine, rather than an all-too-fallible human. At least I hope so.

I continued walking down the street, glancing only casually at the events taking place around me. There Grace was, a few yards away, meeting me, taking in the scene. Except for me, she was by far the most dangerous person on that street.

# 43

## Grace

After a concert Saturday night, he invited me back to his place, where I had never been. His place! I thought, He is ready to remove a major barrier between us. Not one we've ever spoken about, but still it was there. His private space. God knows he had invaded mine. He had always managed to act as if I was the one holding back, but we both tended to keep a lot to ourselves. Symbolically speaking, letting me into wherever it is he lives was really letting me in, I suspected. No more walls.

# 44

## Sam

I made slow love to her that night. It was only the second time. She laughed and cried, at different points. I slid inside her so easily.

And when she fell asleep, again in my arms, I felt almost as relaxed as she. Until a few hours later, when, stirring, I reached for her and felt nothing.

I found her, crying very quietly, wrapped in my discarded shirt, in the bathroom.

"They won't be back, will they?" she whispered tragically.

"Who?" I knew whom she meant.

"I killed them. I really did." She took a shuddering breath. "Do you know what the secret to killing people is?"

"Yes," I said softly.

"They never really expect it. It's not fair, really. They don't."

"Yes." I seated myself on the floor, Indian-style. She had the cover of the toilet down and was sitting on it.

"I can never sit comfortably like that." She pointed at my position. "Except me. I always expect it."

I handed her some toilet paper.

"They can always turn against you, you know."

"Who can?"

"You know. People. When I was little, they used to make fun of the weird kids, and I wouldn't. And then they started making fun of me. Just speak your mind, and they make you pay."

"Not always," I said.

"Yes. Always. I'm just tired of it. I don't want to deal with it anymore. Other people and their feelings."

"You chose a rather extreme way to avoid that," I pointed out.

She just looked at me angrily. I went on: "You know, I have been doing a little reading about serial killers."

"I'm not a serial killer. Are you crazy?" She had stopped crying at least.

"You have murdered four men, that I know of," I said.

"Three men. And one of them was self-defense."

"And what about the businessman you had an overstimulating dinner with not so long ago?"

"I didn't kill him."

I said nothing, but my eyebrows rose of their own accord.

"I didn't. I was going to. I felt it. But then I didn't. I said no. And he stepped back." She was staring beyond me, envisioning the scene again, I imagine. Now I was a bit confused.

"You did not kill him?"

"Don't you believe me? Why would I lie?" Why indeed, I thought. "That's the second time I tried to do the right thing, and the result was the same anyway."

"That is not the proper conclusion to reach. You had bad luck."

"I always have bad luck." She glared at me.

I bit my lower lip to keep back the words. How could I argue that I was good luck for her? I referred back to my thesis.

"Very often, apparently, serial killers are attempting to murder the selves or part of themselves that they want to reject. The man who hunts boys reminiscent of himself, young, weak, lonely, or trusting, for example. A replaying of psychic history."

"I'm not a serial killer."

"Then what would you call it?" I asked mildly.

"I had a couple of psychic breaks," she offered after a minute, triumphantly. "And why aren't you a serial killer?" she asked pugnaciously.

"I am afraid that is just the way it works."

"What's the difference between a serial killer and someone who kills remorselessly and unfeelingly over and over for years?" she pursued, somewhat unpleasantly.

"Perhaps the answer is in the question. Unfeelingly. Perhaps the lack of any feeling about the act puts it into a different category."

"I didn't feel anything when I did it," she said.

"But you did before and after," I noted. "You did what you did because of your feelings. That is the point I am trying to make, however unwelcome it is. I suspect that while you wanted to avoid hurting those boys' feelings, you saw yourself in them. It was you whom you were protecting."

"That's ridiculous."

"What an effective argument." I said nothing for a few moments. She was quiet as well.

"If I'm a serial killer, then so are you," she repeated decisively.

"Does that make you feel better?"

"Do you moonlight as a shrink? I can just leave now, you know."

"I know." I thought for a moment. "Maybe you should go."

"You want me to leave?" She looked about to break into tears again.

"I want you to know that you can. . . . And you can come back."

"I don't want to go." She sniffed.

I could not help smiling, even as I shook my head. "There has to be something for you between saying yes and murder," I said slowly. "That something is saying no. I think you must keep trying."

"No."

"Did that feel better?"

"No."

"All right. That is quite enough of that."

"No."

"Grace."

"What? You said it."

"I think we should go back to sleep."

"Did we solve anything?" She was smiling a little bit now.

"Yes. I am a serial killer and an armchair psychoanalyst, and the latter is the less forgivable of the two."

"Well, it's nice of you to try," she said. I just looked at her. We sat there for a little while longer; then I took her hand and we shuffled slowly back to bed.

# 45

## Grace

It had been a week since I had seen Sam. We talked on the phone every day, though. We were in production at the magazine—long and late hours.

Audrey had been nosing around my workstation quite a bit for the past few days, asking questions: What had I been up to lately? Was I okay? I seemed a little down, she said. She assumed I was upset over the horrible accident I had witnessed, which was true enough. She was being uncharacteristically concerned. It didn't take a genius to figure out that she was just digging for information in general, experimenting with a variety of tactics. She was still harping on Pete's disappearance. I had zero time for that. How was I supposed to get any work done? I answered her queries with barely any thought.

"Well, where do you think he is?" she tried at one point, just casual.

"I don't know," I said evenly, rifling through some of the countless papers on my desk. "Where do you think he is?"

"He seems to have fallen off the face of the earth."

"Well, maybe he did. Maybe he alienated some Peruvian he shouldn't have. I'm not his keeper."

"You may have been the last person to see him."

"Doubtful. And you're talking like a detective novel."

"Well, this is a mystery to me."

"Men are a mystery to me. Anyway, I'm sure it will be solved someday. Maybe tomorrow when he walks back in."

"I don't think he will."

"Geez, did you ever think maybe he ran away from you? He wouldn't have been the first." It was true; he wouldn't have been. Her jaw dropped for a second. Then she turned away sharply and left.

Wow, I thought. I really got to her, and I wasn't even trying. But I didn't have time to dwell on it, because at that moment, Pete did walk in.

My only thought was, this is what the world looks like when it's coming to an end. Nothing matches. I could see quite clearly through the window behind him that the sky didn't fit with the buildings, and the light outdoors looked completely unrealistic. The clouds ran across the sky in blurry streaks. Or was it me?

Pete spoke.

"I think we need to talk, Grace" was what he said. Oh my God, is he breaking up with me? I thought wildly. I grabbed my head to keep the brains in. And stared at him. He did not look good. There was a nasty-looking scar on his forehead. His hair was matted. His clothes were the same ones he'd been wearing the night I killed him, but they were very dirty.

"Not here," he said definitively.

Audrey had just missed him. Several others, though, saw him there and just stared. I got up from my chair and followed this blast from the past slowly down the hall and into the elevators. He said nothing. We reached the first floor, and he led me out to the little nearby Mexican place where my colleagues and I typically congregated after work, for lack of anything better. It was deserted in the middle of the afternoon. We sat at a table for two and, finally finding my voice, I began to speak, but he motioned to me to stop.

"Just give me a minute. I'm still a little weak."

I looked around the place, thinking that I could still run. Yeah, but could I hide? From a ghost?

The ghost spoke. "Surprised?" he said.

"What happened to you?" I asked, still in awe and not thinking.

"I thought you could tell me."

He sounded different. But, strangely, he didn't sound angry. I think I would have been. Maybe this was bigger than that.

"I don't know what happened after I pushed you into the river," I said simply.

"Then I'll tell you. I was fished out by some homeless guys who were camped out nearby. While I was unconscious, one of them stole my wallet. But several others took care of me. Apparently I was in and out of consciousness for days. I don't know how many. And very feverish. But nothing was broken, except my head a bit. They've got a real interesting little world down there. I just left them this morning. I'm going back with my laptop later."

"I'm glad you're okay," I said. I really was. I couldn't help it. His eyes weren't the least bit mushy or puppy-doggish.

"Really? That's a little strange, coming from you. I mean, I'm a little bit hazy, but the last thing I remember was your hand reaching out in the middle of our conversation and shoving me into the drink."

I hung my head. "Yeah," I said sheepishly. "Nothing wrong with your memory."

"So why'd you do it, Grace? I thought we were having a good time."

"I can't say."

"Sure you can. And I think you'd better."

Part of me was floundering, trying to think of what to say, trying not to think of my future life in prison. But a little part of me couldn't help thinking that I should have knocked him on the head a lot sooner. This was a different Pete. I liked him much better this way.

"I wasn't" was what came out.

"Wasn't what?" he asked, confused.

"I wasn't having a good time," I said miserably.

Surprisingly, he let out a short laugh. "So you decided to try to kill me?"

"I didn't know how to tell you. I didn't want to hurt your feelings."

"What did you think, that I wanted to marry you?"

"Well, no," I said, a little bit insulted. "You just seemed to be really into me. Pardon me, if I misunderstood your intentions."

"Well, boy, you really did. It was just fun. I mean, I wasn't in love with you or anything. If you weren't into it, I'd have been a little bummed, but it wouldn't have killed me. I would have gotten over it in about ten minutes."

"Hey, there's no need to be mean," I said, offended.

"I'm not. I'm just being honest. Like I always am. You could have tried. You could have just said something."

"I just didn't know how."

He looked at me carefully. I tried to look him back in the eye.

"Just between you and me, I think you could use a little help," he said seriously.

"Well, I hear they have therapy in prison."

He sat silently for a minute.

"Look," he said at last. "Did you mean to do it?"

"Well, no, I didn't *mean* to do it."

"Then I'm just gonna consider it an accident."

"An accident? Did that bump on your head unhinge you? You could have died. That was my doing."

"Well, you're just gonna have to work it out yourself. I've got this story on these homeless people to do; then I've gotta get back in touch with the men's magazine people, and then I've gotta get back to Peru. I don't have time for police red tape."

My mouth was agape.

"I'm just gonna leave this between you

and me. And hope you learned your lesson. But I better not find out you're doing it again. Or you'll be the next story I do."

I was still looking at him as if he were crazy, which I honestly think he was.

He started to get up. "Oh, and I'll be sending you a bill for my clothes."

"What about your medical expenses? Plastic surgery?"

"What, are you kidding? This scar looks cool. Improves my credibility."

I reached out and grabbed his arm. "Are you sure? I mean, you have every right in the world to seek justice."

"Frankly, I just don't think we should try going out again." He started to totter out of the restaurant.

"Hey," I called after him. "Audrey was asking after you."

"I'll give her a call," he said, without turning.

After a few minutes, I was able to get up from the table. I managed to snag a cab and get inside my apartment before I threw up.

Then I called Sam.

# 46

## Sam

"Do you want me to kill him?" was my first question, after Grace told me the story.

"Are you nuts? After what he's been through? Don't even think it."

"Apparently the lot of you are crazy" was all I could conclude as I came back into the room after splashing some cold water on my face. "You think he will continue to say nothing?"

"Geez, obviously I hope so. But whether he does or not, he stays alive."

"Not if he meets up with the wrong Peruvians."

"Don't even think of polishing up your Spanish. It's my business. You're not in any danger," she informed me.

"If you are, I am," I said simply.

Her face crumpled. Gently at first, and then with more and more emotion, she began to sob. She cried for a good hour and a half after that.

So I made her tea. I put her in her night-clothes—that is, a T-shirt and sweatpants she had lying around. I held her and supplied her with tissues. This abandoned, limitless sobbing was something I had not seen from her before. The pullover I was wearing was becoming quite wet from her tears and her nose. At one point, she noticed and started to apologize.

"I'm ruining your sweater," she said.

"That is what dry cleaners are for," I told her.

At last, and almost predictably by now, she began to speak.

"I feel so relieved. And so guilty." She sobbed. "I'm just crying. It feels so good. And you're taking care of me. You'd even kill for me. Not that you should," she reminded me, "but the offer is nice. I know you mean well. I just always tough every-thing out alone, you know? And here you are helping. Nobody ever does that. I don't let anybody do that. I just haven't been taken care of in a long, long time. But I can take care of myself," she added hastily. "I was doing okay all alone, wasn't I?"

"Well, in a manner of speaking. Everybody could use a little help."

"You are so sweet," she wailed.

"I am not sweet."

"I'm sorry, I just can't stop. It feels so good to cry. And you don't mind."

I patted and stroked her back lightly. Like the end of a rain shower, she gradually dried up.

"You know? I can finally rest with you. It just seems like I don't have to worry. I'm just so tired of worrying about everybody's feelings. Even mine. You can worry about mine. I mean, not all the time. Just now and then."

"Now and then," I repeated, soothingly, I hoped.

She was silent for a few minutes, reflecting. "I don't know if I'm good or if I'm bad," she whispered to me after this pause. "But I feel . . . strange. Not afraid." She blinked. "Free."

I held her tightly. She felt free. I did not. Not anymore. For me, that was an improvement.

## 47

## Grace

Killing people changes you. It does. It can't help it. I don't know myself anymore. Or maybe I know myself better than I ever did. But I don't know what I will do. I was angry when I killed those guys. I know that much. And now I can't always keep it in. Sam once told me that when he works, he knows it's either his life or the other guy's. And there's a certain freedom in that. Losing the old fear makes me a little afraid of what I might do.

I got into an argument with someone at work the other day over something I would normally swallow. Instead, I went up to my coworker and stated my case, told her why I was offended and why she was wrong. And I won. She apologized. I went back to my cubicle. I should have been satisfied, but I wasn't. I wanted more. Once you open that door . . .

I guess I was angry when I did the things I did. I thought I meant well. Really. I'm not sure killing is such a sensational solution to the hostility problem, after all. I'm not sure what is. But I don't want anyone else to pay for my problems anymore. Unless they're causing them, of course.

# 48

## Sam

She found me in overdrive. The not-unforeseeable outcome when one opens one's home to someone. But then, I knew the risks. She kept her finger on the buzzer, attempting to rattle me, until I let her in the front door. That left me with perhaps a minute and a half—while she took the elevator up to the floor I lived on—to put away my playthings. Too late, I realized that I would have to add a little device to the lift to disable it when I wanted to slow someone down. She was knocking on the door as I slid the last gun into its hideaway.

"So, how's tricks?" she asked. She was a little breathless.

"What do you mean?" I parried.

"What are you doing? You look like I caught you in something naughty."

"Impossible," I declared.

She walked around the living room, suspiciously. She finally came to my laptop. That was really an oversight. I was still on-line. Peter's motor vehicle history was on the screen, complete with address. Rather damning, I am afraid.

"So what you say to me means exactly nothing, is that it?" She turned to me angrily.

"You were too upset to be logical."

"I said no. No, no, no. When is that word gonna work for me?"

"He was hardly in a rational state when you spoke. What he said cannot be relied upon."

"No. What you said cannot be relied upon. I actually trust him."

"I have to do as I see fit. As long as he is alive, he can change his mind. I do not relish prison visits, nor can I guarantee that I could risk them."

To my utter shock, she pushed the computer off the table. It hit the floor, beeping a few times before giving up the ghost.

"I'm mad at you," she said. But she looked a little afraid of what she had done.

I walked across the room to her from where I had been standing by the door—

slowly, carefully, both palms up in a gesture of pacification. How angry is she? I thought. Even more to the point, I wondered if she was armed. Grace stood her ground. I reached out a little tentatively, took her hands in both of mine, and led her to the nearest couch, seating myself as I pulled her gently down to face me.

"I have to kill him. I know you understand why."

"You have to kill. But not him. You touch him and we're finished." She was shaking; I could feel her tremble.

"You cannot mean that. That is insane. He is not worth that."

"It's not about him. It's about you and me. If I can't trust you, then forget it." She was serious.

I let go of her and leaned back on the couch, pressing my hands to my eyes. My head was beginning to ache. I had never had this kind of discussion. I had been fairly resolved on a faux mugging. There was not time enough for any complicated, more subtle procedure. With my eyes closed, I could see exactly how it would proceed. The look on his bewildered face before he crumpled to the ground, a bullet in his brain. It was necessary. And because of that, it was as it had been before I met her. It was beautiful.

I opened my eyes, and she was still sitting there looking at me. Clear-eyed. She spoke more softly now.

"There's no such thing as a purely reason-able killer. Is there? You can't be adjusted in every other way and still heartlessly kill people."

"I have to say, I have no idea," I endeav-ored to answer lightly. "But I think I am a touch too old to change my spots." Although, privately, I was beginning to have a few doubts on that score.

"What is it you like about killing?"

"I never said I liked anything about it. It is a job."

"Yeah, and it was war. But it's over. What are you, one of those Japanese soldiers hid-ing in the jungle for twenty years?"

"War never ends," I argued, rather weakly.

"You like it," she replied, pressing me.

"I like control," I said, giving in to her interrogation. "I like precision. I like the sim-plest solution possible."

"Then how come you like me?" she asked.

"It is against all my principles."

"You're gonna have to come up with a bet-ter word than that."

"Can it not just be that I am evil? Or natu-ral? Perhaps I am the natural state of man. Before scruples or neuroses are imposed."